UNDER THE VULCANIA

UNDER THE VULCANIA

MAUREEN FREELY

BLOOMSBURY

First published 1994
Copyright © 1994 by Maureen Freely

The moral right of the author has been asserted

Bloomsbury Publishing Ltd, 2 Soho Square,
London WIV 5DE

A CIP catalogue record for this book
is available from the British Library

ISBN 07475 17150

10 9 8 7 6 5 4 3 2 1

Typeset by Hewer Text Composition Services, Edinburgh
Printed in Great Britain by
Cox and Wyman Ltd, Reading, Berkshire

CHAPTER ONE

She wanted to be aroused, not awakened. Not treated with care, but shaken, just to prove the existence of a core. She wanted to be unwrapped, and because she had fallen back to sleep after the first muted alarm, her wish came true. She dreamed she was a package. She dreamed she was being jostled by a pair of unseen hands, turned upside down and shunted backwards and forwards as these hands struggled to remove the ribbon, as they ripped the thick, noisy paper with the nervous roughness of ill-restrained curiosity, and opened the box, and plunged into the tissue paper, first pressing it for some indication of the shape of its secret, then tearing it apart layer by layer until the light began to filter through, first gently, and then suddenly with such harshness that it annihilated all shadow. Now a face was peering down at her, a face so close and so large that she could not begin to recognize its owner. 'There seems to have been a mistake,' it was saying, 'There's nothing in here. Nothing at all.'

Fiona opened her eyes. The light coming in through the windows was, though weak and white, too much for her. She made to turn away from it. As she did so, her feet struck against something that she knew at once to be her breakfast tray.

For no good reason, because she had no grievances to nurture, she felt like kicking the tray off the bed. As always, she restrained herself, and instead sat up, rearranged the pillows, turned off the alarm before it could sound again, placed the tray on her lap, drank down the thimble-full of juice, poured herself half a cup of weak tea, surveyed the pills next to the toast, and glanced at the disconcerting picture of happiness in the mirror on the wardrobe. Who was this china figurine eating breakfast in bed and why was she smiling?

She could hear her husband in the bathroom, shaving at the basin. Turning off the water, he called out, 'Are you awake, dear?'

'Just barely,' Fiona said, in the half whisper that was in danger of becoming her natural voice.

'I'm on my way downstairs. Can I bring anything up for you?'

'No. Please. You've done enough already. I'm sure I could have gone downstairs for breakfast. Just tell the children I'll be driving them to school.'

'There's no need for you to overtax yourself. I can easily drop them off on my way to the hospital.' He emerged from the bathroom as he fastened the buttons on his fresh blue shirt. Then he looked up at her, his smile somewhat undercut by the sad clinical knowingness of his gaze. She tried, out of fairness, to detach herself, to see him as a stranger might see him – admire him as a specimen, for his bones (fine), his complexion (olive), his eyes (large, dark), his muscle tone (admirable), his manner (bedside at its most professional). It didn't work.

'No,' she insisted. Now, as an unjustified rush of claustrophobia threatened to overtake her, it was all she could do to maintain that half whisper. 'Darling. You must try to give me the benefit of the doubt sometimes. I'm better now. I'm not going to have a relapse. Let me take the children to school for once. I've thought about it and . . .' Hating herself even as she did it, she paused for effect. 'It's what I want.'

It's what I want. Even today, how many women in the world could claim that as their magic formula? As she got into the clothes she had selected and he had laid out for her the previous evening, as she brushed her thick curls and slipped into her shoes and headed slowly down the spiral staircase, she surveyed the felicitous results: this house she had gutted with the blessing of her generous, if somewhat calculating husband and then rebuilt according to her own, capricious lights, combining styles that did not belong together, rebelliously mixing incompatible patterns and colours, inventing optical jokes that made a mockery of the dignified exterior . . . only to find her originality praised – and even worse, imitated – by the very people she had hoped to insult. It was a palace of socially acceptable subversions, this house. From top to bottom, it was a whim come true, a repository of half desires she had long ago outgrown. But no one, and least of all its other occupants, seemed to see this. No one had ever complained about the wrongheadedness of its decor, the impracticality of its layout. Try as she might, she had never managed once to offend a single sensibility. This failure had (or so Fiona secretly suspected) sealed her success as an architect.

And even her success as a mother – if the ends justified the means. But weren't they too well-behaved these days? Couldn't that be the most worrying sign of all? When she joined her family in the kitchen, she was almost sorry to see her sombre thirteen-year-old son stacking his cereal bowl so obediently in the dishwasher. She almost despaired to watch her serene ten-year-old daughter adjusting the ribbon that held back her long, sleek, perfectly brushed mane of chestnut hair. What went on in their heads? she wondered. Did they have any idea what went on in hers?

More to the point – did her husband have any idea? From the wise, forgiving smile with which he now greeted her, it would appear he did. 'Sit down, dear,' he said as he pulled out a chair. When she had done so, he gave her a doctorly pat on her back and said, 'I can't tell you how good it is to see you back in your old place at this table.' He was a good man, she reminded herself. A devoted parent. A consistent and uncomplaining provider. Once, long ago, he had been the fatherly lover she then required, but now . . . He made her blood run cold.

It was the sharp morning air that revived her – and the children, too. They had a brief argument about which radio station to tune into. They complained that she wasn't aggressive enough in the rush-hour traffic. 'You used to be a demon,' they reminded her. She was pleased that they remembered. Daniel had a sneezing fit. Ruth caught him trying to wipe his hands on his shirtsleeve and called him a name. He made as if to hit her. She screamed. He called her a name. Fiona sighed with relief.

She offered to drive Daniel up the last hill to his school. He said no, that he preferred to walk. Ruth explained afterwards that this was because he was afraid his friends would laugh at him if they saw him getting out of a baby-blue Mercedes. No chance of getting noticed, though, by the double- and triple-parked mothers outside Ruth's school. They were refreshingly hostile as they struggled to look as if they were accommodating each other.

The sun was just breaking through the mist as Fiona found her way out of the gridlock. The houses on the hill on the other side of the valley went from grey to pinkish gold. And just as suddenly, out of nowhere, a whim was born. A whim that could – she knew at once – easily turn into something more perverse.

Would she? Could she? She pulled to the side of the road to check her diary and her shopping list. Yes, she still had ten days to get ready for that competition. Yes, even the urgent household chores could wait. They could do without curtain sashes, shoelaces, and six fluted wineglasses for one more day. The lunch she had scheduled she could shift with a phone call. Jacqui would be more than pleased, she suspected, about the suggested change of venue.

She signalled to go back into the traffic. When a man in a painter's van paused to give way, she thanked him with a smile that was, she thought afterwards, a bit too forward. He took it demurely, as a comment on his good looks. As she swung off to the left at the next crossroads and he to the right, she asked herself, would he have done the same thing if he had known she was on her way to the Vulcania?

CHAPTER TWO

How serene it looked on its sculpted hilltop. How blankly it presided over its bare circular drive. It was baldly majestic in the way that only a recently renovated Art Deco monument could be. If only . . . if only . . . but such thoughts did not pay for shoes or groceries, Raul reminded himself as he guided his small motorcycle to its designated hiding place. This was a precaution he did not need to take, but in a job like this, it took on a certain symbolic importance. It comforted him to begin each day by covering his tracks.

A pair of puppies were at play outside his office window. The spectacle of their awkward, innocent antics provided a welcome, if only intermittent, respite from the jumble of order forms on his desk. Fifty pounds of oranges, twenty-five cases of California sparkling wine, five reconstructed sunbeds, one hundred and seventy white roses, seventy-nine ten-ounce bottles of massage oil, all urgently required . . . and for what? He despaired as he surveyed the memo marked 'Today's Appointments'. The Department of Health – again. What did that mean? Two training seminars. Three interviews. The lawyer. A prospective investor, and a policewoman for lunch. All this and who could tell what else to fit in with his usual unending string of personal consultations . . . and all of it depended on his own ability, apparently never questioned by his gullible clientele, to turn in an impeccable performance. How long could he keep it up? He found the answer on his desk, in the school portraits of his four young and beseechingly devoted motherless daughters.

The phone rang. As he reached for the receiver, he recomposed his face. 'Raul here. How may I be of assistance?' It was the night manager coming off duty with his routine report. As they ran through their list, Raul watched the last stragglers from the night shift drift past his window. They looked as if every muscle in their bodies ached: a few were even limping. And there, beyond the row of willow trees, waiting to clock in, was the morning shift – all freshly showered biceps and tight jeans. At nine on the dot, the servants' entrance swung open to admit them, while in the car park beyond, the first customers were already emerging from their cars.

CHAPTER THREE

Two were carrying briefcases. One had a string of toddlers in tow. Most had sports bags and squash racquets. As they milled around the foyer, waiting to be registered, the usual things happened. Women with children of similar ages clustered together, continuing whatever forgettable conversation they had begun the day before outside the school gates. The toddlers climbed on the leather furniture and tugged at their mother's arm. Two long-lost acquaintances recognized each other, crying, 'What are *you* doing here?' – and slightly annoying the sharp-featured woman who was standing between them and trying to talk into a mobile phone.

Meanwhile, behind the front desk, Gretchen and Mariella were busy double-checking appointments. Mariella was wearing a Mao suit. It

11

made her look too butch – Raul would have to talk to her, but later. Now there were other things to attend to ... all details, but details that he knew, from experience, could assume monstrous proportions if neglected. 'I assume you are already aware that Sam, Elliot, and Jimmy won't be in until after one,' he said to Gretchen. 'They said they had exams. I'd appreciate it if you or Mariella could check up on that for me – after the rush, of course. And also, Douglas has called in sick with a toothache. Check with this dentist for proof of treatment.' Raul handed Gretchen a piece of paper with a name and number on it. 'If you like,' said Gretchen, as she glanced up from her computer screen, 'I can check this dentist's credentials, too. All too often, they turn out to be bogus.'

Raul nodded. 'Good idea. You can't be too careful with these students.'

'It's just the age,' said Gretchen.

'Yes, but unfortunately, this happens to be the age that's most in demand.'

'I can't see why,' said Gretchen. 'Although of course the clients don't have to listen to their Neanderthal small-talk.'

'In our line of work,' said Raul wistfully, 'there is no substitute for stamina.'

'An overrated virtue, if you ask me.'

'That, my dear Gretchen, is because you inhabit one body, not fifteen or twenty.'

'I'm still not impressed. Women can go on indefinitely – unlike even the most vaunted of our little princes here.'

Raul could feel his eyelids dropping involuntarily. 'As you know only too well, Gretchen darling, women can pretend.'

Moving off in the direction of the control centre, he said over his shoulder, 'I'll be wearing my bleeper if you need me for anything.'

Gretchen nodded absent-mindedly as she returned her attention to the computer screen, and Raul continued his rounds. The control centre was problem free. The squash courts were full, mostly with pairs of women. Only one mixed game was in progress – Raul checked the coded programme notes posted outside and then peeked briefly through the window to make sure everything was going according to schedule. Half of the morning shift was in the weights room, and the observation deck was packed. As he made his way past the clusters of newly arrived clients, he tried not to pay attention to their comments, but their voices carried: 'Will you look at those thighs.' 'Hmmm. That's my idea of pectorals.' 'I'm not even going to say what I would give to get my hands inside those shorts.' He was glad to reach the comparative tranquillity of the Annecy Annexe.

Here, in the main hall, Romero was taking the other half of the morning shift through the last floor exercises before warm-down. Next door, in the kitchen offices, the caterers were in a small buzz because the new secretary had lost the list of RSVPs for tonight's birthday party. That meant that they didn't know how large to make the cake. As Raul quickly established, they were conducting their search for the list on the wrong computer drive. They thanked him effusively for rescuing them from disaster. He reminded them, perhaps too crisply, that he was simply doing his job.

He moved on to the clinic. The matron, a burly, deep-voiced woman in her late forties, was waiting for him at the door. They went over her schedule, which included fifteen routine checkups and two STD seminars. 'So let's hope we don't have any emergencies today, because I simply don't have time for them.' She informed him that the latest blood tests for the new job candidates were back, with all but one result being satisfactory. 'Would you like me to break the news to the poor lamb?' she asked. She assumed a superiority in such matters. She did not know that he had once worked as a doctor. 'No,' said Raul. 'You'd better leave that pleasure to me.' He hated such phone calls. It didn't seem fair to the boys to be hearing news of such gravity from a prospective employer ... and yet it would be irresponsible to pass the buck ...

How depressing it was to be a manager. In the end this was what got him down, and not the fact that he had drifted so catastrophically far away from his true profession. He was glad to take temporary refuge in the crèche, where the toddlers were busy banging on an assortment of drums and the older children engaged in a free-for-all in the foam-rubber pit. One child was catching her breath in muted sobs as a nursery assistant read her a story-book. How trusting this child looked, how grateful, how free of the corrupting contortions of preening desire, and yet this was a girl, and one day she would ...

Enough, enough. There was no sense in putting it off any longer. The time had come for the personal consultations. He headed for the salon, where (he checked the list posted next to the door) he had sixteen scheduled clients waiting, as well as one last-minute appointment whose first name was all too familiar to him.

It was . . . could it possibly be . . . Yes, it was.
It was . . .

Why would she?

How could she?

CHAPTER FOUR

The salon had three sections. To the left of the entrance was what could best be described as a boudoir. Here a team of hair-stylists and cosmetic advisers were caring for the last remaining overnight guests – in other words removing all trace of their evening of fun and returning them to the hard, varnished look so popular among successful career women. To the right was one of the Vulcania's many dress boutiques, each of which had the Creative Billing Option that had been one of Raul's first and most brilliant innovations. As he had so accurately predicted, many clients who shared bank accounts and credit cards with their husbands found it convenient to pass their entire day bill off as an impulsive dress purchase. Fewer questions were asked this way, and less suspicion aroused, as overspending on clothes was thought to be typically feminine and therefore unworthy of interest.

This particular boutique specialized in items to be worn *in situ* – lingerie, poolwear, catsuits and even evening gowns, along with an assortment of role-playing costumes for rent. There was a seamstress on hand to take orders and measurements for any shape or design that was out of the ordinary. As Raul walked in, she was making the final adjustments to a nurse's uniform. 'Now there's no need to carry it around with you,' she was saying to the client. 'We can have it waiting for you downstairs. If you give me your appointments card, I'll take down the correct cubicle number.'

'Actually,' said the client, 'unless I am mistaken, I reserved a showroom.'

'The one with the stirrups in it, I assume?'

'Yes, that's the one.'

A wave of music drowned out the rest of the conversation. Paul Simon, moaning about how much it scared him to be happy in love after all these years. Huh, thought Raul. Then he caught sight of his face in the mirror: it was, as *she* had told him so often, the closest human equivalent to the storm cloud. What had she called him when he was in this mood? Yes, now he remembered: Haughty the Hawk.

He recomposed himself. Having checked the results in the mirror and found them only just passable, he moved with feigned and carefully monitored good cheer into the central area of the salon, where Fiona and sixteen other women were waiting in their swivel chairs. A stranger walking in right now would have had no trouble assuming that they were waiting for their favourite – if alarmingly high-tech – hairdresser.

Some were examining their make-up and/or wrinkles in the mirror. Others had their elbows propped up on the counter as they watched the promotional video on its built-in screens. A few who knew exactly what they wanted were already punching in their orders. All the women were dressed in the silk pyjamas that came with the price of entry.

While Raul worked his way down the line, Fiona idly perused the catalogue they had given her, noting, as she flipped through its pages, how high one's standards got when the prey looked so willing. What *did* she want today? And with whom?

She eavesdropped on the two women sitting to her right.

'Did you see the one in the rowing frame?' said the stiffly coiffed blonde to the close-cropped redhead.

'Yes, but it says here he can only take afternoon bookings.'

'Maybe we can double up.'

'Simultaneously, or in the same half hour?'

'I suppose it depends on how much you want, plus how many preliminaries.'

'Hmmm . . .' said the other. She pursed her lips as if she were inspecting the ingredients of a box of detergent. Fiona tried not to smile, as she knew this woman to be one of her husband's patients – while her friend, who had either not recognized Fiona or else did not wish to acknowledge her, given the circumstances, had, until several years ago, been the art teacher in Fiona's son's school.

She had left, as Fiona recalled, to have a baby.

What, then, was lacking in *her* life? Fiona was unable to listen in for further details because now she felt a pair of hands on her shoulders. Looking up into the mirror, she saw the Monsieur staring intensely down at her reflection. Seeing him so close, it seemed to her that she knew this disdainful, hawklike face from somewhere . . . except . . .

He picked up a brush and passed it through her curls. 'So. It has been a long time since we've seen you here.' So that was all it was, she thought to herself. A *déjà vu* with an alibi.

'Yes,' she said. 'It must have been, let's think, fourteen, fifteen . . .'

'Seventeen months,' he said briskly. 'I checked the records. It was, I should add, before my time.'

Which meant that she knew him from somewhere else, not here.

'What can we offer you today?' he now asked.

'I'm not quite sure,' she said. 'I thought I'd buy the usual necklace.'

'The twelve-bauble necklaces are fifteen per cent off this morning, and if you checked the board or the video, you may have noticed that we are also offering a number of specials.'

'To tell you the truth, Mr . . .'

'Call me Raul.'

Raul, she thought. Raul.

'Raul, to tell you the truth, the special offers didn't spin my wheels.'

'I see.'

'No, please, don't take it the wrong way. Actually, I was hoping you would be able to help me. My own ideas don't seem to be good enough. Or rather, even if it is a good idea – as many of your offers here are – it somehow loses its attraction because I know exactly what is going to happen from the very start.'

'You sound bored with life.'

'Do I?' said Fiona, somewhat taken aback by the intensity of his tone.

'I'm sorry. That was unprofessional. What you are saying to me is that you would prefer to have your schedule arranged according to the discretion of the management.'

'That's sounds about right.'

'Actually we have a name for it. La Piñata. We offer it as a regular service but only recommend it to clients we feel are sufficiently self-possessed. The form is for clients to pay at the end, and only to the degree that they are satisfied, but I'm warning you, it can be expensive.'

'I'm not worried about money.'

'Then I take it you married well, after all.'

'Actually,' she said, bristling slightly, and so failing to bear in mind that he was overstepping his role. 'I did so happen to marry well, as you put it, although I would certainly have no trouble supporting myself on my own salary.'

'Forgive me,' he said. 'I didn't mean to pry.'

'I have nothing to hide, although that's hardly the point at the moment,' she said. 'After all, this is my day off. I take it you think I'm up to the challenges, financial and otherwise, of La Piñata.'

'It's your decision. I would never dream of

trying to influence you,' he said. Again, there was that edge to his voice. Why?

'Let me escort you to the towel room,' he said. 'We have changed the layout slightly since your last visit. And oh yes, there's the insurance waiver.'

'I already signed one at the desk.'

'Yes, but for this you need an extra one.'

Why? she wanted to ask. For the first time since her arrival at the Vulcania, she felt a shiver of apprehension. 'This is not to say that you are in any real danger,' he assured her as he stopped in front of a computer terminal to order the required print-out. Could he read her mind, too? 'You retain your veto power. All you need to do is pull one of our emergency cords. I assume you remember what they look like.'

'Yes, of course,' she said.

'And I'm sure I do not need to add that I am easily reached should La Piñata fail to please.' Now he was sounding almost mocking. Or was he issuing an invitation? If so, an invitation to what? There was no way of reading his signals, so she chose to ignore them. She left him to tap his cryptic commands into his computer, picked up her towels from the towel-room attendant and headed down the warm, low-lit, perfumed stairs towards the Roman Baths.

CHAPTER FIVE

The Roman Baths were made up of eight small rooms and an observation deck, all looking out on to a colonnaded open-air marble pool. It was fed by the city's famous hot springs: hence the steam rising from the surface and the unusual opaque blue-green tint to the water. The room into which Fiona had descended was an enlargement on the idea of a shower stall; the subtly positioned spigots in its marble ceiling, floor and walls were programmed to provide all new arrivals with a calming aquamassage. Clients could choose both the rhythm and the intensity of the water flow on the control panel at the back of the glass closet into which they were meant to put their towels and personal effects.

What possessed Fiona to take her aquamassage without bothering to remove her silk pyjamas she did not know. It was one of those things that just happened and turned out to be a better idea than she could ever have imagined. She liked the way the warm, wet silk clung to her skin, the way it responded to the always changing pulsations of the water jets. The way it rounded her curves, wrapped around her nipples, and evaporated the angles that had grown so much harsher since her illness.

For some reason – what? – a memory came back to her, a memory that couldn't be more distant from her present surroundings. It was a memory from that summer so many years ago, when life was so very different, when she had worked for that co-operative, picking water-melons. Succumbing to thirst on that first day in the sun-baked field, she had broken one open, for the juice. Having sucked in its sweetness, she had found herself only thirstier . . . As she stood now amidst the water jets, she opened her mouth and let the hot spray tickle her tongue and hit against the back of her throat, the warm droplets moisten her lips. The sensation was just as sweet, just as tantalizing . . . she could not bear to break the mood, so when she retired to the adjacent steam room, she left the water running. She told herself she needed the sound . . .

Her towel was a rich royal blue, but the

steam was so thick that she could see it only intermittently. It was like lying on a beach in the tropics and searching for patches of sky between billowing storm clouds. The heat embraced her in its usual forceful manner as she reclined on her elbows on the lowest of the marble platforms. The wet air caked her throat. Breathing required such concentration that she didn't immediately notice the pair of hands resting on her shoulders.

She arched her head back to see who had claimed her. She could see nothing but steam. As she hunted for a gap in the folds and creases of the steam, she felt the hands sliding downwards, now passing over her nipples, and now returning, back and forth, back and forth . . . she arched her head even further back as she strained for a glimpse of their owner, and as she did so, the hands took hold of her breasts and squeezed them, so hard and so suddenly that she could not help but cry out . . . but no sooner had the cry left her lips than she felt someone else's lips, an upside-down pair of lips, touching her lips, and a tongue probing their shape, licking her teeth, and then flickering against her tongue and then withdrawing, to suck her lips away from her while the hands pumped her breasts, pinched her nipples and pushed their way downwards, fumbling at the buttons and pulling at the elastic of her silk pyjamas, reaching

26

for her inner thighs, now pinching, now caressing them, now travelling up to her breasts again, and now back to her shoulders and then disappearing again into the hissing clouds of steam.

First she sat still, waiting. Then she looked over her shoulder. Nothing. She probed the steam with her arms and met with no resistance. She sat forward with half an idea to move on – only to find the hands emerge out of the steam in front of her and push her roughly back.

Now both hands had grabbed the elastic of her silk pyjama bottoms. Now they were ripping them apart at the seams. Now a tongue was making circles around her clitoris, now it was thrusting into her cunt. Now, as it returned to her clitoris, she opened her legs and thrust her pelvis towards the invisible tongue, which by now had turned into a pair of lips, a pair of lips that sucked her so hard she lost the capacity to resist it . . . and now, as she found herself on the edge of surrender, when she would have said yes to anything, the tongue and the lips and the hands suddenly withdrew . . . she lay on the marble slab, gasping, and listening to the hissing steam as her heart pounded. One thousand, two thousand, three thousand, four . . . it had been a minute now at least, now two, and now three . . . was that all there was to be?

She stood up and made to look for her towel, but suddenly the pair of hands had grabbed hold of her again, and had pushed her down on the marble slab, while a second pair of hands roughly separated her legs. She could see a dark shape mounting her, feel a thick penis thrusting into her, once, twice, three times . . . it kept pumping and she lost count. Now she felt two tongues working on her, one for each nipple, and each one following a different logic, and a different rhythm. She gave in to them both, and opened up to . . . what?

In the control centre, Raul surveyed the act on his closed-circuit television. His eyes were cold, his expression stiff with disapproval. So this is what she likes, he said to himself, who could ever have imagined? Then he reminded himself, ruefully, that he had. So then why was he surprised – he, who knew better than anyone what ice maidens liked best . . . with a sigh, he typed out the instructions for the next event on her morning agenda.

But even as he entered the command, the image overtook him, seeping out, as it were, from between the lines, the forbidding and paradoxical image of perfection she had been that first day so many, many years ago when she had walked

– twenty minutes late but unapologetic – into his study.

How could he begin to justify the anger he felt for her today if he thought about his own sorry and self-willed decline? Wearily, he turned away from the flickering computer and dialled the Central Locker Room on the internal videophone.

Roland, the deputy-on-duty – or rather, a faint and soft-edged image of him – appeared on the screen. 'Would you mind getting me Winston?'

'Give me two seconds,' Roland replied. He disappeared from the screen to be replaced by an indistinct sea of restless, half-naked bodies, all conversing in loud, jocular tones that were none the less impossible to decipher.

When Winston came on the screen, Raul said, curtly, 'I'd like to co-ordinate our readings. But first of all – since the steam obstructed my view somewhat – I'd like to confirm that you kept to the script and that yours was the only penetration.'

'Yes, sir,' said Winston.

'Give me your ETD,' said Raul.

'I put it at three or four minutes.'

'You're not far off. I logged you at two minutes, twenty-four seconds. I have your charts here, and handicapping those, I estimate that you won't be ready for your next performance until 11:15.'

'If you don't mind my interrupting, sir . . .'

'Go right ahead.'

'Well, sir, I was sort of counting on doing five performances today.'

'Why?'

'Well, sir, because I'm going off on my internship come June, and I'm short on resettlement money.'

'What course are you on? I've forgotten. Remind me.'

'Electrical engineering.'

'Yes, of course. And where's the internship?'

Winston named a large industrial centre in the north.

'You do know that our chain has a subsidiary member up there for which I would be happy to write you a recommendation.'

'That's very generous of you, sir, but . . .'

'Don't tell me. You were hoping to go straight. Don't apologize, Winston. It can happen to the best of us. Well, in that case, all I'll say is that I'll put a note here stating that you wish for five performances per day shift. But I'll still have to base my decisions today on the bottom line. Your ETD could do with some improving. Have you been keeping to the regimen?'

'I eat oysters for breakfast, if that's what you mean.'

'What I meant, of course, was a balanced diet, eight hours of sleep per night, a mile a day in the pool, and private intercourse kept to a minimum.'

'I do my best, sir, but my girlfriend doesn't know what I do for a living, and so there are times when I'm forced to keep up appearances.'

'It's never a good idea to lie,' Raul said sharply. 'Especially not to a woman you're serious about. What will you do if you walk into a cubicle one day and find her waiting for you? It *has* happened, you know.'

'Yes, sir, I know, but meaning no disrespect, sir, I'm not too concerned about that eventuality, because she just isn't that kind of girl.'

'Well, don't say I didn't warn you,' Raul said curtly. He switched off the videophone, but it didn't do him any good. He still hurt as much as if Winston had punched him in the stomach. Not that the boy had meant any harm. Not that the boy had any idea how arrogant he was in his innocence. As Raul moved back to his desk, he shrugged his shoulders and reminded himself that there was no insurance. Everyone gets fooled once – and then gets to spend the rest of his life acting . . . professional.

For once, the prospect was comforting. He was happy to divert his attention to the dilemma of the client in number forty-five, who claimed now that she had specified apricot and not strawberry yoghurt for her body meal. And the client in number fifty-four, who was not happy with Alan, and wanted Brian before lunch or else . . . except that Brian, as usual, was fully booked. Meanwhile, there were the trainees waiting for him in the dummy room, and as he prepared to go over to speak to them, he wondered if the best solution wouldn't be to try a few of them out on the floor that afternoon. Not only would this solve a few of the logistical problems created by the staff shortage, it could also provide them with a hands-on learning experience that could prove useful for class discussion – and himself with a much needed respite.

But there was no escape from the object of his dissatisfaction. As he headed for the disgruntled clients in numbers forty-five and fifty-four, he almost collided with her, an apparition not in white now, but in green, as he walked past the swinging doors leading from the Roman Baths.

She looked refreshed, transported, and in a curious way, absent.

She looked straight through him.

CHAPTER SIX

Sprawled on a sofa in the Day Beau Centre, Roland watched this same scene from the protective distance afforded by its one-way mirror. Something was not right between this woman and his employer: he could tell from their body language, and few people could read body language as fluently as he. This – he felt, but would never have the audacity to say – was what made him such an invaluable Deputy Monsieur. The Vulcania would go under in a day without Raul's taut and scrupulous management, but Roland was the one who tended to the human side of things – by which he meant building up morale amongst the beaux, anticipating emotional crises even before they happened, and counteracting the pressures of the job with the right combination of banter, heart-to-heart talks, and recreational diversions. Without these discreet services, the Vulcania would not be a place worth working.

It was, in a strange way, the most rewarding ministry he had ever had. And again, this was a thought he kept to himself. He assumed that Personnel had chased down his references but there was no sense alarming his charges unnecessarily. It was enough to have been rehabilitated. He didn't want to have to prove this to all comers every single working day. It was enough to know that here, for once, and possibly because of the treatment he had received in prison, he had a clear idea of his role. Which was not to say he had anything approaching a reliable formula.

This morning, for example, there was Winston to get back on track. Whatever Raul had said to him on the videophone, it had sent him into a mood. They had all been watching this woman in green who had come so very close to colliding with Raul on her way to the juice bar. They had all seen her accept a menu from the most achingly beautiful specimen of manhood the Vulcania had to offer without even looking at the body attached to the hand. When two of the younger beaux began to fantasize about what they would like to do to her, Winston scowled in his dark and irresistible way and told them to cool it.

'You still haven't figured it out, have you?

They're the ones who'll be having you. And what they take out, they don't bother to put back.'

Too true, too true, Roland agreed silently – but some people were less well equipped than others to deal with the facts, and the pair Winston was addressing were among the most fragile. Shaw, for all his vulcanic good looks, flawless musculature, and loud posturing, was painfully sensitive about his recent low ETD scores. They were probably due to too many betablockers. He had been informed and counselled on this: having sworn off them, he was bound to show improvement in the next set of league tables. Meanwhile, Roland had had to go to some lengths to make sure the current set did not become common knowledge. He had also had to cover for the other one, Wing, but in a different way, because Wing was nothing if not a good performer. But this had created problems for him in his everyday life. Having gone through an unusually long honeymoon period thinking this job allowed him to get what he wanted most out of women and get paid for it, he had finally figured out how he was being used. As far as Roland could figure out, he had been reading Marx and misapplied the ideas to his own situation. Now he thought all women, even his girlfriend, even his classmates, wanted one thing out of him and one thing only, and he protected what was left of his virtue with the tenacity that even a turn-of-the-century chaperone would have thought excessive. His problems were compounded, Roland was sure, by the fact that he had the features – and the body – of a Greek god.

He needed to be reminded – and this was what Roland was trying to do now, and why he had to find a way to counteract Winston's cynical comments – that a job like this could, if handled properly, be a positive learning experience. There was an up side to the newest profession in the world. After all, it provided much better money, didn't it, than the usual student jobs in libraries and restaurants. And the hours – weren't they so much easier to fit into a busy schedule? As for the social side of things – he was sure that the boys made far closer friends working in this environment than they did anywhere else. And sometimes, if a powerful client took a special interest in a beau, he could find himself with a patron for life. As he had been saying only yesterday to Sonny, there was more than one way to use a casting couch, but in putting it so boldly, he had been tempting fate, because now the phone rang, with a warning from reception about one of the most powerful clients of them all.

'Just to let you know that a Mrs Magenta has just booked in. We didn't let her have her usual first choice and she didn't seem to mind about that, but bearing in mind that tag you left on her file, we thought we ought to let you know.'

'Thanks. I'll warn Sonny. I can see him from here. He's on duty at the juice bar.' He put down the phone, moved briskly over to his computer, typed out a command to have Sonny removed from juice bar duty, frowned at the message that came back. He bleeped Raul, whose stern face appeared on the videophone seconds later. 'You can't have Sonny for La Piñata, at least not for the juice bar,' Roland told him. 'It's too risky. That woman's back, and she'll be stalking him, and she might make a scene.'

'Why has she been allowed in at all?' Raul asked.

'It's a little difficult, if all you're going on is a bad feeling in your bones, which is all I have. And if the suspect happens to be a well-known journalist, it's even more difficult. Just a little! All I felt I could do was leave a note saying no bookings with Sonny.'

'If you're going to remove him from the juice bar, you'll have to make sure the person you replace him with fits all the specifications for the task at hand.'

'Will do,' said Roland. But even as he had the computer do its search through the available-beau roster, he knew – in his bones, as per usual – that there was no one who came near to Sonny, not by any yardstick, not by a mile. As much as he hated Madeline Magenta and everything she stood for, he couldn't fault her for her taste. How could Raul have been so insensitive as to place their most valuable asset in such a vulnerable position? The least he could have done was agree to have him removed to safety before and not after they found a replacement. Some things were more important than keeping up the façade of smooth management. And who was this woman in green anyway? Why was she so important? Why had she been allowed to breeze in at the last minute and demand a service that usually required forty-eight hours' advance notice? And on top of all that, here was Raul working overtime to make sure she had the Vulcania's top talent.

Roland was tempted to get Raul back on the videophone and get him to level. But then, as he glanced over his shoulder and through the one-way mirror at the juice bar, he saw it was already too late.

CHAPTER SEVEN

When Fiona was a child, her favourite games had all involved pretending that the world around her was in some way a hoax. On trains and other moving vehicles, she had been in the habit of closing her eyes long enough to convince herself that she was travelling backwards rather than forwards. Left to her own devices at home, she would walk around the house ignoring her feet. The thrill was the threat of putting her foot out and finding no floor where she expected it to be and falling down the stairs. But the best game of all – and the one that had seen her through any number of tedious schooldays – was to elaborate on the idea that she was the only living person on earth and that all other humans were apparitions placed there to amuse her and keep her from feeling lonely.

That's the way she felt now as she sat on her swivel stool with her back to the bar, enjoying a glass of thick, chilled mango juice, surveying the simulated rain forest around her and the domed, vaulted pink marble pool whose crystal clear water now lapped at her feet. From here she had, as close as she could get to it in this underground labyrinth, a panoramic view. Despite the lack of natural sunlight, the atmosphere still managed to have the fresh, sleepy slowness of early morning. The only people in the showrooms to the left were cleaners – bona fide cleaners with bona fide hoses – while to the right in the Appearance and Reality Centre, the Figures of Fun waited patient and immobile in their parking bays. The only noise emerging from the thickets of tropical greenery was the warbling of canaries, and the occasional shriek of a minah bird, and, every time someone walked through a concealed and far-off set of swing doors, the crack of a whip and the faint moans of a client on the rack.

Suspended over the pink marble pool in a net hammock, two women dressed in G-strings were fondling each other. They were employees – you could tell because they were smiling fixedly, as if for an audience, and because their movements were too graceful to be anything but choreographed. In the water below, a cluster of young, golden-haired men – also employees, by the look of it – were struggling to jump high enough first to touch them, and then, when they had achieved that, to overturn the hammock. The women cried with feigned dismay, then managed to rock the hammock hard enough so that it swung beyond their reach. Catching hold of a trapeze, one managed to swing to the safety of a treehouse, while the other, having clambered on to a pole, now tried to rejoin her mate via a tightrope. Pretending to trip, she found herself swinging from the rope by her feet. The golden boys swarmed around her, reaching up to catch hold of her breasts, but no sooner had one of them done so than she dropped head first into the water and disappeared. Her pursuers dived in after her, but for nothing – already she was back with her friend and mocking them from the poolside.

Another well-rehearsed drama seemed to be going on at the juice bar, between the barman (who looked as if he had stepped off a billboard advertising low-tar cigarettes) and a tense-looking woman in her mid-thirties. Fiona would have mistaken her for a client had it not been for the wooden way in which she delivered lines which no real-life woman would be caught dead saying, or at least not caught dead saying in a melodramatic whisper in public. 'I can't believe what you're telling me,' she was saying. 'What kind of woman would want that kind of thing anyway?'

The only words Fiona could make out in the low rumble of his response were, 'You've just got to accept that this is my job.'

'Then why wouldn't they let me book you?' she insisted. 'If this is your job, I should be able to have access to you like anyone else.'

'Listen. I'll have a word with the desk and see what I can do about that. In the meantime, I think the best thing would be if you went off to the jacuzzi or something and cooled off.'

'How the hell am I supposed to cool off in a jacuzzi?'

'Listen, I was just making a suggestion. Because I think if you stay here, you're going to get upset. Because I'm going to have to get back to work, or else I'll be out of a job by lunchtime.'

'And you think that would make me unhappy?' she wailed as he walked away from her.

'I'm sorry,' the barman said to Fiona, 'I'm just going to have to ask you to ignore her.' So, Fiona thought. She was supposed to be the third to make a triangle. She wasn't quite sure she wanted this.

'Down to brass tacks, then,' said the barman.

'What'll it be? My brief here is to give you whatever you want. It's on the house, and I mean literally.'

'Do you have to say it so sincerely?' the other woman wailed.

'Just pretend she's not there,' the barman said to Fiona. 'That's what I'm doing. She's just jealous, and do you mind if I tell you why? It's because you're too beautiful. This must happen to you all the time.' He reached across the bar and passed his hand through Fiona's hair. 'You don't mind if I say that to you, do you?'

Would it matter – would it alter his masklike smile at all? – if she told him she did mind? She neither wanted nor needed such play-acting. She got plenty of that at home. What she wanted now was . . . just to sit here with her chilled mango juice and feel it make its thick, icy way through her hot, parched chest, and luxuriate in this sense of being out of her body without dwelling on the degradations she had engineered for herself in order to gain this degree of detachment. She just wanted to BE here, and not think about it, but when she opened her mouth to tell him so, the words that came out were entirely different.

'I want to suck your cock,' she said. 'And I want you to come over here and sit on this stool while I do it.'

In less than three seconds he had vaulted over the bar. She stood up, went over to his stool, took his thick penis out of his shorts, kneeled down and went to work with the confidence only known to actors who have become their parts. Although she took pleasure in the swiftness with which it changed from soft flesh to a hard and impatient rod, her detachment remained – she knew it was a character performing, and not herself. But what was the play, and how had she come to be so familiar with it?

She could not see the woman at the other side of the bar, but she could hear her angry breathing, and the nervous tapping of her fingers on the wooden counter. 'Now that you have me big and hard,' said the barman, 'what do you want to do with me?'

'I want you to lift me up on the bar,' she said. 'And then I want you to suck me off until you can't bear it any more and then I want you to fuck me.'

In seconds, she was on the bar with her green silk shift hiked up above her breasts, her legs falling to either side while he kneeled to service her. As she wrapped her hands around his head, she closed her eyes and tried to pretend no one was watching her, but of course she enjoyed listening to the laboured breathing of the actress on the other side of the bar, and she delighted in the discovery that she had another witness to her depravity when she next opened her eyes. This was a man in early middle age who seemed, if anything, more upset than the woman by the sight of the barman preparing to enter her.

'You don't have to take it all the way, Sonny. And under the circumstances . . .' The man was interrupted by the woman, who shrieked, 'Get them to stop!'

'I can't!' Fiona found herself gasping. What a slut I am, she said to herself, and with that thought, she came . . . and came . . . and came . . . until he came, too.

Rather too quickly.

He climbed off her so gracefully that she began to wonder if he hadn't had ballet training. 'That was great,' he said. 'That wasn't work, that was a pleasure. Listen, I still have some time. What would you like me to do for you next?'

'Nothing,' she said, slipping off the counter. 'Go back to your jealous friends.'

'Maybe you'd like to meet later, then. After lunch sometime. How about that?'

But before he could recite any more lines, she had stripped off her green silk shift and dived into the pool.

It was just the right temperature. As she glided

in an effortless arc, first towards the marble pool floor and then upwards towards the bubbling turquoise surface, she felt herself being washed clean of all the little doubts that had begun to fasten to her like barnacles. Why do I need this? Why do I like it? Why does it please me even more when people watch, when the men who are probing my body are lying through their teeth? As she climbed out of the water, she left these questions behind her. Refreshed, she helped herself to a thick white towelling robe from the pile on the top marble step. She fell back into a reclining chair, wrung the water from her hair, and directed her attention to the Appearance and Reality Centre, which was now springing into action.

A woman had activated three Figures of Fun. From this distance and in this light, they looked almost human. It was only the diaphanous afterglow that identified them as holograms. They were talking – it was impossible for Fiona to make out the words. All she could hear was the supplicating tone. One by one they approached the woman with outstretched arms. One by one, she walked through them, each time laughing more maniacally, more triumphantly, than before.

* * *

'Note this scene well,' said Raul to his twenty trainees as they clustered around the one-way mirror. 'What you see before you is the logical extension of the industrial revolution. Let me put it more bluntly. Consider yourselves as workers who run the danger of being replaced by the miracles of technology. Look. Here, already, we have holograms that can satisfy desires beyond the physical abilities of any red-blooded man. See before you a woman too angry to be satisfied with the normal role-reversals our establishment was originally set up to provide. If you are to keep one step ahead of technology, if you are to focus on the services technology has not yet managed to identify, you must first understand your target audience. What do you think brought this woman to this point?'

He looked to his trainees for suggestions — none was forthcoming. 'It's surprisingly straight-forward,' Raul continued. 'Our subject is simply doing to these holograms what she feels men have been doing to her. This is what we call tit-for-tat wish fulfilment. It is common amongst women who have not had the opportunity even to identify, let alone explore, their deeper needs. And that, I put to you, is where you must look if you are to stay in employment. You must watch her, try to figure out what she wants that she herself has not even dared to imagine . . .'

Again, he surveyed his trainees, noting with sadness that their eyes had glazed over. Then he turned back to the one-way mirror. To his dismay, the holograms had been abandoned. The woman had run over to the poolside and was now effusively greeting Fiona.

Thank God their voices did not carry.

CHAPTER EIGHT

The woman's name was Jacqui, and she was
Fiona's lunch date. Her Appearance and Reality
session had given her the intense euphoric rush
that is only known to the desperately unhappy.
Only two hours ago, she had been crying next
to her phone, and trying to keep herself from
making yet another hang-up call to her former
lover's wife. She was not proud of the driving
urge to hurt this woman, who had needed all of
three weeks to spirit the disputed party back into
her clutches – but that didn't make her hatred
any easier to control. Nor, for that matter, her
continuing passion for the undeserving man in
question. Just before Fiona got in touch, Jacqui
had turned to soul-searching – what was wrong
with her that men kept dropping her like this?
Two years into her divorce, did she no longer

have what it took to be a desirable partner? What was the point of living if you didn't have anyone to share your bed? Now, as she strode confidently along the side of the pool, she counted her new-found reasons.

'What a good idea it was to come here!' she exclaimed to Fiona. 'I haven't been for ages. Have you ever done A and R? No? Well, I couldn't recommend it more highly. It has put me into *such* a good mood I can't begin to tell you. I just wish I could hire one of those guys and keep him with me all day long.' As Jacqui made herself comfortable on a neighbouring reclining chair, the A and R Centre sprang into action once again. But all this new customer wanted to do was engage her half dozen holograms in a disco dance. 'Honestly,' said Jacqui, 'sometimes you despair of the female imagination.

'Not that I'm planning anything particularly daring for myself today,' Jacqui continued. 'I hope you don't mind, but I've booked myself into the Chastity Beltway. I decided that was what I needed most, although maybe it's just how they put it in the catalogue: "Not just learning to say no, but learning to *enjoy* saying no." When I saw that, I said to myself: Righteo, Jacqui, that is exactly where you are emotionally at the moment, so why deny it?'

It was true, so true that Fiona hardly dared nod in agreement.

'But I haven't copped out one hundred per cent,' Jacqui continued. 'I've left the last hour open with the option of a visit to the Halfway House. They have a few new specials going there. I might try out the Virtual Reality Challenge.'

'What's that?' Fiona asked.

'Well, basically, there are two black boxes. One offers sex with a real man, and the other offers sex by simulation. I think you have to wear a special suit – I'm not quite clear on that point. Or maybe you're blindfolded. Anyway, after it's all over, you get to guess which one was the real thing, you know, just like the Pepsi Challenge. But to tell you the truth, I'm not sure I'm even up to that. In the meantime,' she said, as she picked up her briefcase, which looked so incongruous in these surroundings, 'what I was going to suggest was that you come up to the Beltway some time around one.'

'I can't promise to get there exactly on the dot,' said Fiona. 'I don't have a watch.'

'Don't worry,' said Jaqui, 'I'm flexible, and so is room service.'

51

CHAPTER NINE

There *was* one clock Fiona could see from her reclining chair. Technically speaking, it wasn't a clock at all but an intermittent digital hologram. Once every five minutes, it swept its way around the entire labyrinth, gently reminding those with busy schedules that time was money, but sweeping past so quickly and quietly that those with time or something even better on their hands need not even notice it.

Now it said 11:05. Watching it emerge from the rain forest, dance briefly on the surface of the pool, and then dash up through the rainbow fountain towards the swimming channels, Fiona decided that to follow it would be just the way to fill her time between now and lunch. Once again, she dived into the perfect water. It was just cool enough to refresh and cleanse her, and just warm enough to assure her comfort. She headed into the spray of the rainbow fountain. After swimming through the tunnel of water, she found herself in a dark, warm cave, at the far end of which was a landing stage, where a man sat ready to dispense inflatable rafts, pedal boats and small canoes. In the past, Fiona had always preferred canoes, but this time she decided it would speed her up too much. And she wasn't in a rush. She opted for a raft.

Out she went into the Gardens of Babylon. Here the marble floor of the swimming channel sloped upwards gently on both sides to meet with narrow sandbeds that were themselves edged by a thick, low-lying foliage. The twists and turns of the channel created coves, which contained water fountains and resting places of differing shapes and sizes. Half a dozen yards beyond this meandering strip of greenery were the showrooms, where the usual mundane dramas were now in progress.

In the first, a client was lecturing a classroom of men who were dressed like aviation students. She was wearing nothing but a black lace bra, net stockings, and a matching suspender belt. In the next showroom, a man dressed up as a surgeon was climbing on to an operating table to have sex with a client who was pretending to be either dead or unconscious. In the third, a client dressed in an evening gown was masturbating while two men dressed as construction workers on imitation scaffolding outside the window struggled to gain access. In the fourth, a customer dressed up as a turn-of-the-century maid had just lifted her skirts to reveal to the man in the fourposter bed that she wasn't wearing any underwear, while in the fifth, a client dressed in a schoolgirl's uniform was also lifting her skirt while the man at the desk marked Headmaster was rounding the desk with his arm raised up to spank her. In the sixth, yet another customer dressed as a *circa* 1947 housewife was saying goodbye to the postman just in time to welcome the milkman ... Honestly, Fiona thought to herself as she drifted past, what *was* it about uniforms?

How could it possibly be exciting to play through a scene you yourself had devised? Where was the risk? The surprise? As Fiona approached the first jacuzzi, she was happy not to know what the three men sitting in it had in mind for her. It added zest to what would otherwise have been an uninspired conversation about a recent oil spill in the Pacific. When after five or ten minutes, none had made advances, she said her goodbyes and moved on.

The one with the long, jet-black pony-tail

caught up with her just as she was rounding the next curve in the swimming channel. He pushed her raft on to the bank, clamped his hands on her upper arms, and without waiting for an invitation, straddled her. His penis was already stiff and large as it bobbed over her unparted legs. 'Don't even try,' he growled as he let go of her arms. Reaching into the leather pouch strapped to his waist, he removed a condom which was textured in such a way as to make his penis look like a reptile. Without further ceremony, he pushed her legs apart and thrust himself into her. The strangeness of his appearance and the warmth of the surroundings sent her quickly to the edge of climax, but as she basked on the brink, her mind raced away from her, first to the man she now realized this beau reminded her of – the second or third stranger she had ever picked up – and then to the seedy Spanish bar where she had been working that summer – not strictly for the money, because she had more than enough to last her until she took up her internship in the autumn – more for the pleasure she got out of degrading herself by almost but not quite doing it for money.

But now her brave new whoreboy was drawing her back into the present by pounding his great ribbed reptilian cock against the back of her cunt.

'You like this, don't you?' he was saying as his pumping grew more rapid. 'You could do this all day, couldn't you? You've missed your vocation. You could have been an A-one slut. I'm telling you, lady, whoever you are, you make me feel like I'm the one who's paying.' He thrust into her so hard she let out an involuntary yelp. 'That's right. Cry for help. But don't worry. No one's coming to the rescue. It doesn't matter who's paying now. I'm the boss around here. I'm going to come now and there's nothing you can do to stop me. Why should I worry, anyway? It's what you want.'

She had no secrets from this stranger, she thought, and she exploded, the involuntary ecstasy first vibrating her cunt and then radiating outwards. He knows, she thought, as she felt his penis pumping, and then, as he withdrew, leaving her too limp to change her position, she asked herself . . . how?

It was a question she had occasion to ask herself again, further along the swimming channel, when she came upon the tennis court.

By now she had managed to stem the tears that had come, without apparent explanation, as she escaped from the cove of her previous adventure. For some reason, she had felt compelled to leave in a hurry. It had been some minutes before she realized that she had, in her haste, forgotten the raft. This discovery distressed her far more than it ought to have done. Then she had grazed her leg against the side of the channel. The grating sand between her leg and the channel had produced a minor scrape – it was this that had propelled her into racking sobs. She had felt as if she were mourning a death – but whose? This is what she asked herself as she lay flat on her stomach in the safety and seclusion of this new cove from which she could just see, between the clumps of bushes (the terrain being tamer here – not so much subtropical as country club), this reassuringly mundane tennis match.

Reassuringly mundane, but at the same time strange. Because who could have guessed that she would meet in such surroundings a scene so reminiscent of her childhood? Two men were playing. A third was watching. She noticed now that they were older than most of the beaux she had seen so far. Not too old – they were in their mid-thirties, just like the men she had watched as a teenager the summer she took up nude sunbathing.

She helped herself to a new towel, which she arranged in a place that gave her some – but not quite enough – privacy. As she lay down on her stomach and closed her eyes, she listened to the steady rhythm of the tennis match begin to falter, as, increasingly (she knew without looking), the players trained their eyes not on the ball but on her naked body.

It was very warm here – as warm as she remembered that other day to have been, that first time she had indulged in this game as a teenager. Now, as then, she pretended to be offering herself up to the sun and not to their greedy, disbelieving gaze, as she turned on to her back and bared her swollen breasts. The volleys grew shorter and more lopsided and then extraordinarily long, almost mechanical, as she again pretended to put her own comfort first and turned back on to her stomach.

'I'm worried about your skin,' she heard a deep voice say. 'I hope you will allow me to rub in some oil.' It was one of the tennis players. Without waiting for an answer, he dribbled the oil on to her back and then massaged it in, first concentrating on her shoulders, her arms, and the nape of her neck, and then going steadily lower, now kneading her buttocks and her thighs, now prodding the gap between them . . . gently but firmly he rolled her over on to her back. She felt him rubbing the oil into her breasts, her stomach, her upper thighs . . . while on the other side of the bushes, the match continued.

How much could they see? she wondered as her masseur entered her. Enough to see what she was good for. Enough to see that she pushed herself up against him with his every thrust, enough to see that when the rhythm took on a life and a logic of its own, she locked her legs around him, so that he could penetrate even deeper, so that when his packaged penis began to throb and release its poison, she could forget without any effort that it wasn't going anywhere, she could imagine it spreading out through her entire body.

They could see this, she was sure — enough so that when he stood up and adjusted his tennis shorts, already self-sufficient, already avoiding her gaze, she felt so limp she didn't know if she would ever be able to move again, and so was unable, even unwilling to object when the second tennis player appeared before her.

His massage she found even more of a comfort than the first. When he entered her, she felt complete again. When she felt his penis pumping inside her, she felt once again alive. Or was it a drug? So wrapped up was she in her own ecstasy that she did not notice when this man climbed off her and the third tennis player climbed on. Every time she looked up, it seemed, there was a new, unfamiliar face. Meanwhile, the mechanical volleys continued in the tennis court, while sleepily

she asked herself, what am I trying to prove?
Why am I here, making the same self-indulgent
mistakes I first imagined more than twenty years
ago? Whose idea was this? Why?

CHAPTER TEN

'If all kitchens were as clean as this one, I'd be out of a job,' said the health inspector, as he snapped up his briefcase.

And if all jobs were as easy as keeping a kitchen clean . . . 'We try,' said Raul, but even he could catch it now – this mocking edge that threatened to undermine the polite informalities. When he and the health inspector reached the door, he was careful to give him an affable smile with the handshake. He turned away content that he had safeguarded his neutrality – and dreading the woman who was the next item on his agenda.

Her name was Miranda Simpson and she was a junior partner in the law firm that represented the empire of which the Vulcania was only a small, if much admired, part. There was nothing particularly wrong with her – it was, rather, what she represented. He found her above ground in the – the name still made him wince – the Institute for Continuing Research on Our Bodies, Our Genitals.

She was just beginning her tour of its bogus facilities. Her guide was the so-called Institute's self-appointed director, Jane Fanshaw, who was, by a very long shot, Raul's least favourite staff member. Jane had what he had once called a seminar voice. She was stretching it to its outer limits to give unmerited weight to her rap. This, he noted, had grown more outrageous than ever.

'Our starting point,' she told a desperately nodding Miranda, 'is the idea that most women objectify their bodies. Everything we do in here is designed to get them to take back ownership of their private parts. We start with tactile experiences that you, Miranda, probably associate with early childhood.' She pointed to the room where a group of women were playing with clay.

'Actually,' Miranda said, 'I was doing that until just a few years ago. Before I went into law, I went to an art and design school.'

Jane Fanshaw nodded brusquely. 'And then there's the Sensual Quarter. Each room along this corridor specializes in a different stage of educational massage. Mark One is automassage excluding genitals. Mark Two is sister massage –

that means women pairing up – also excluding genitals – and then Marks Three and Four are auto and sister WITH genitals.' Turning to Miranda, she added fiercely, 'We have no truck with the concept of the G-spot here – in case you were wondering. What we do have' – here she threw open a wide metal door – 'is a Specularium.' She led them into the small, stuffy domed room. It called to mind a planetarium, except that the image beamed on the ceiling was the interior of a vagina. 'I'm not sure if you're old enough, Miranda, to remember the speculum. Well, in the early seventies, we used them fairly routinely for self-examination. They were useful little gadgets, but personally, I prefer this larger cousin.' She gave a little kick to an apparatus the size of a sixteenth-century Ottoman cannon that a rather worried-looking woman with a modified beehive hairdo was straddling.

'AND', Jane now said, leading Miranda and Raul back to the reception area, 'we also offer what we call Body Talks. These are sessions in which all communications must be made non-verbally, i.e. through mime and tactile contact. This seems to be the experience that opens people up best to the possibilities of change.'

'And does that result in return custom?' Miranda wanted to know.

'We have follow-up support groups, if that's what you mean.'

'No, actually I was making a bottom-line sort of question, if you'll excuse the pun. What I meant was, what percentage do you get relaxed enough to use the facilities downstairs?'

'I'm not sure I follow you,' Jane said in an ominously calm voice.

Just in time, Raul's bleeper went off. He excused himself, dealt with the call – a routine head count – in the hallway. When a rather flushed-looking Miranda emerged two minutes later, he took her straight along to the video theatre to see the tapes that were the main reason for her visit.

She had to determine whether they could be productively used as evidence in a paternity suit filed by a former client. It didn't look like the case was going to hold water, because, as Raul now told Miranda, all four visits the petitioner had paid to the Vulcania during the period under review had been taped and showed the beaux doing everything by the book, even though the petitioner was trying to trip them up every step of the way. In one she tried to bite the condom while she was giving him a blow-job. In another, she pretended she herself was wearing a polyurethane shield. In the third, she encouraged him to enter her unprotected and then withdraw before coming, and in the fourth she subjected him to a tantrum in a baby voice when he refused not to use a condom. Then she topped it off by withdrawing to a corner and sucking her thumb.

Her ploys were not in any way out of the ordinary – Raul saw them every day. In fact, they were so standard as to feature in his lecture on precautions for trainees. But when he showed the videos to Miranda, he could tell that they shocked her.

'I think we could make a case for the petitioner being deranged,' she said in a voice she tried to keep from sounding shaky.

'You could,' said Raul, 'and you could probably get away with it. Unhappily, these episodes you've seen are not uncommon, and so between you and me, we cannot dismiss them as abnormal behaviour – just regrettable.' He realized too late that young, straitlaced Miranda was in danger of taking this comment as a slur on womanhood.

'It may just be that this kind of establishment attracts that kind of psychosis,' she suggested.

If only, he thought wearily, the problem were that simple.

'In any event,' she continued, 'we only need these videos as back-up. The DNA testing should be sufficient, so long as we can track down the fifth man. Have you had any luck?'

'We've traced him to a bank in Hong Kong. He was not particularly happy about our contacting him – now that he is an executive, he does not like to be reminded of this particular chapter of his life. And he was not – I should add – particularly co-operative.'

'But you said he was Chinese.'

'At least half Chinese, anyway.'

'Well, the baby isn't, so that may end up being enough.' She scribbled something down on her notepad, then checked her list. 'There's a suggestion from on high that perhaps DNA testing could be part of the induction procedure, so that we have the necessary information at source. If we did that, we could avoid such tracking problems in future.'

'It's quite an expense,' said Raul, 'but if they don't mind paying . . .'

'Another suggestion was double sheathing.'

'We tried that, but it lowered the average ETDs drastically.'

'ETDs?'

'Excuse me, it stands for Estimated Time of Delivery.'

She still hadn't twigged.

'Of sperm.'

She blushed. 'Oh well,' she said, attempting a nonchalant laugh, 'I guess we'll just have to wait with our fingers crossed until science comes up with a painless and one hundred per cent reversible vasectomy! Or even, I suppose, medically induced retrogressive ejaculation. Which brings me', she gasped, 'to the last but possibly most important item on my shopping list. The senior partners have expressed concern about the UI Centre, because the legal problems it could present if things went wrong are truly monumental. So I am supposed to give them a report as to standard operating procedures, hopefully to quell their anxieties. I personally am ideologically predisposed to the concept, but I thought it would help if I could see it first hand while I'm here.'

'No problem,' said Raul as he rose to escort her. But he knew it would be.

There were, to begin with, the places they would have to pass on the way. The Ice-Cream Parlour, which catered to women who liked vanilla sex. The Rough Trader Saloon, where the racks were just the beginning. The Halfway House, for clients who couldn't bear to see who was giving them pleasure. If he showed her the dual monitors – the one on the left-hand side showing a row of women only visible from the waist up, lying on cushioned slabs and gyrating at various rates while they perused magazines and idly filed their nails, and the one on the right-hand side showing a row of young, muscular, and terminally exasperated men pumping away at the same women, here only visible from the waist down – what would she say? And what would she make of the neat little row of confessionals, abuzz with fantasies so bizarre that he sometimes wished he could transmit them straight to the police station and get their inventors locked up. Not to mention the Casino ... if Miranda thought all women were good and nice, how was she going to explain why some women only seemed to feel good and nice when they were treating themselves or someone else as objects? He could sense her disapproval as they made their way down this corridor of perversities. He could almost hear her lame attempts to reason it through – that at least it was no longer just men who were writing the scripts ... at least it was better that women with such tastes indulged them under these ultra-controlled circumstances, instead of at home in front of the children ... at least women had a chance to explore their darker natures now ... at least they had choice ...

But it was, as he had predicted, the Unofficial Insemination Centre that perplexed her the most.

How to explain the true affection so evident in the three couples sitting with their arms around each other in the TV Room? Why, if these women wanted to know the fathers of their prospective children, didn't they choose these fathers from their own set of friends or colleagues? Why, if they didn't want to share the parenting, could they not resign themselves to the anonymity of normal, by-the-book, artificial insemination? As for the argument that Unofficial Insemination was more natural, more personal, and therefore more meaningful – how could these women delude themselves like this when every smile, every caress their partners offered, they offered because they were being paid to do so?

Raul watched the shadows pass across the lawyer's face as Pam Killian, the Centre's manager, gave her a quick tour of the facilities. She could hardly look at the warmly furnished bedrooms, or the bulletin board, covered with photographs of the newborn results of previous unofficial inseminations ... when she caught sight of another, smaller bulletin board that featured two or three recent weddings between beaux and former clients, she positively shuddered. 'And what's this for?' she asked, moving quickly into the adjacent lock-up freezer. 'This is where we store the donor sperm,' Raul explained. 'And that's for blood tests. Given the present technology, it's our best possible back-up procedure. It serves several purposes, the most urgent of which is, of course, disease control. As you already know, our beaux are routinely tested, as well as being trained to observe the safest possible practices. But you can't be too careful, especially since there is a three-month lag between the possible time of a virus transmission and a patient showing up HIV positive. So we test our unofficial donors after every session. Although it takes some time for the results to come back, they still do return in time for the receptor to decide what to do about any confirmed pregnancy that may have resulted.'

'And you think that this procedure absolves the management of responsibility in the event that she goes ahead with a high-risk pregnancy?'

'That's what we've been told.'

'How about guaranteed three-month isolation for donors? Or a male chastity belt?'

'That would add considerably to the cost. And you tell me, you're the expert, but I could see both innovations turning into civil-rights issues.'

'Let's say I do a double check on that.' She jotted something down in her notebook, and then looked up and asked, 'And what about this sperm bank?'

'Yes, well, it frequently happens that a woman

who has gone through one successful unofficial insemination will decide two or three years down the line that she wants a sibling. If we've banked the first child's father's sperm, she'll be able to have it inseminated artificially in the event that the father is no longer in our employment. Which is generally to be expected after a gap of that size, seeing as most of our beaux are full-time students.'

Miranda Simpson raised her eyebrows, and then blushed.

'I know it sounds strange, but many of our clients say that they choose this service so that they have a sense of the father's personality, and a visual memory of his features. And if that is what they want, then there's no need for any further physical contact. Once is enough, in other words.'

'Well, I suppose I should say that once is certainly enough from a legalistic point of view,' said Miranda as they headed back down the corridor to the control centre. 'The possible repercussions are bad enough as it is. I bet you see modern birth technology in your nightmares.'

Raul felt his eyelids growing heavy as he gave her what he hoped was a polite smile. How to explain to this woman that the problems presented by modern birth technology were nothing, compared with the logistical headaches presented by the numbered cubicles they were now passing, where clients went to enjoy the closest this establishment offered to good, old-fashioned bordello sex? Even here they had to do their best to draw things out with an array of theatricals. If they didn't, the typical client would be able to run through a normal-length bauble necklace – and put twelve good men temporarily out of commission – in less than half an hour. Almost all the innovations Raul had put into practice since his arrival had been designed to move away from the previous manager's ruinous system of charging a standard fee per ejaculation, and it was only thanks to these efforts that the Vulcania had gone into profit. He might be a failure as a husband and an aid worker, and a poor excuse for a father, but at least he was good at something . . .

But no sooner had he begun to congratulate himself on his professionalism than he saw, seated at the far end of the juice bar, what he first thought could only be a terrible apparition. A woman, dressed in fatigues. A woman, with long black hair and dark angry eyes, who was the picture of his deceased wife, Wilhelmina. The picture of Wilhelmina, that is, that he tried not to remember – when he thought about her, when he talked about her to his four motherless daughters, the image he liked to conjure up was the Wilhelmina of their early, happy days, the days when they had shared the same aspirations and ideals without knowing yet that she had it in her to live up to them, while he didn't ... That early Wilhelmina had a glow to her, and a softness, whereas the Wilhelmina he now thought he saw at the juice bar looked like the woman who had been too angry to say goodbye to him the day she had driven off into the mountains to meet the landmine that would be her death ... this apparition now staring at him from behind a tall glass of mango juice had fire in her eyes, and oozed contempt for the sorry specimen he had proved himself to be ...

He slackened his pace as she rose to her feet. As she headed for him, he stopped in his tracks. It was only when she had passed him that he realized that she was neither a ghost nor his wife come back to life. It was just someone who resembled her slightly. Just another rich, bored client pretending to be a freedom fighter ...

CHAPTER ELEVEN

Except that she was not just any client. She was Madeline Magenta, the crazed journalist who was in love with Sonny. After the unfortunate midmorning episode involving La Piñata at the juice bar, Roland had done some damage limitation: he had booked this obsessive an hour's massage with Sonny at three in the afternoon. But now, as he looked up at the console in the day beau locker room and watched her make her way through the simulated jungle in her army fatigues, he was beginning to have second thoughts. It would not be wise to leave the two of them alone. She could be armed. She could, when no one was watching, attack him with a knife. Roland shuddered, then looked over at Sonny, who was taking himself through a series of casual, confident warm-up exercises as

74

he listened to Roland's morning rap group for low achievers.

They were all new boys just coming out of their honeymoon period. The level of aggravation was high enough for Roland to have decided to bend the rules a little and permit them a shared joint. The most distraught new boy had just finished his first three-hour stint as a beau confessor. He had been deeply disturbed by the fantasies the clients had confessed to him. Two had involved sex with animals – a goat with horns and a baby donkey. Another three had involved incest – with daughters as well as sons. And a good five had culminated in castration – by truncheon, by scissors, by teeth, by hanging, and through the agency of a hungry giraffe.

'It's horrible, but you get used to it,' Sonny assured him. 'After a while you realize that it's nothing but talk, and after that you stop listening.'

Another, who had been having the usual problems performing straight cubicle intercourse, interjected here to say, 'I just can't deal with the games they play. The double binds. You know, I go in there and they tell me they want me to take control, but then, if I do, they resent it, they start yelling at me, and calling me all these names, and telling me to stop . . .'

'And then, if you do stop,' said another boy, 'they threaten to report you!'

'I know. It's perverse,' Sonny agreed. 'But after a while you figure out ways to get around it . . .'

'I've figured out plenty of ways around it,' said a third boy. 'The problem is, my dick's not impressed. I can be acting my head off, but if I can't get a hard-on . . .'

'That's another thing that you learn with time,' Sonny told them.

'I can't believe it. Maybe with the younger ones, but with the . . .'

'The client's appearance becomes less and less important,' Sonny explained to them. 'What you learn to do is to turn yourself on by thinking how sexy you yourself look. You learn to turn yourself on, and, you know, think of yourself as God's most amazing gift to women . . .'

'How the hell do you do that?'

'Easy. You pamper yourself between sessions. Get Roland here to do a little massage. Admire yourself in the mirror. A few organic chemicals don't hurt,' Sonny said, as he reached out for the nearest beau to pass him the joint . . .

It was almost a reflex for Roland to glance up at the console to make sure their privacy was not about to be invaded.

He was glad he did.

'Your lunch guests are here,' Roland informed Raul when he joined him in the middle office five minutes later.

'What do you mean guests?' Raul asked. 'I was expecting one. Leonie.'

'Well, she's brought her best friend.'

'Terrific. That's just what I needed to round off my morning. Well, they're going to have to wait a few minutes. There's no way around it.'

'Don't worry,' said Roland. 'I gave them our new catalogues and they're thoroughly engrossed. Although, if you ask me, it's an elaborate cover. They're hot for each other. I could tell from the moment I laid eyes on them.'

'Well, then, let's leave them to it, OK? In the meantime, there are some major disasters you and I have to figure out how to deal with or else. Let's start with Showroom Five,' he said, tapping the monitors. 'I thought we were agreed that we were only going to use soft bondage materials with that particular fourposter bed.'

'That's what we agreed, yes.'

'Well, this morning someone used handcuffs, and they made gouges in the wood that are going to cost us a fortune to repair.'

'Do you have any idea who the culprit is?'

'It's either Andy or Simon. I'd appreciate it if you would speak to both.'

'Righteo,' said Roland. He swung over to the computer and typed himself out a note.

'And so on to disaster number two. That Neanderthal. George. Apparently he had unprotected sex this morning. It was very embarrassing. When he came in here to talk to me about it, I still had the lawyer whatshername in here taking notes on the paternity suit.'

'Oh my God. Did she work out what the problem was?'

'I understand he spoke to you about it first,' said Raul.

'Yes,' said Roland. 'He came to me as soon as the wicked deed was done. He claims the client wanted it that way. He was very surprised when I explained that his protection was as important to us as her protection. He doesn't have this STD thing worked out at all.'

'You've put him on probation, of course.'

'Yes, for three months, and pending tests.'

'If he turns out to be a financial hardship case, you can put him on eunuch duty.'

'Well, to tell you the truth, I already did, but as we both know, he doesn't have very much upstairs and . . . he misunderstood me. I mean, it was a classic. He actually screamed and cupped his hands over his privates and jumped back, saying, "I'm not that desperate!" The poor guy actually thought I was going to chop his dick off!' Roland laughed at the memory. Raul tried but did not succeeding in joining in.

'He's clear now about what you meant, though, I take it?' Raul asked. 'We don't want him selling his misunderstanding to the papers.'

'You can rest assured that ever since that other misunderstanding last winter, I've been doubly careful when dealing with pea-brains.'

'Not to mention customers with imaginations too large for their constitutions. On the subject of which,' Raul said, tapping another monitor, 'I'd like to arrange for a pulse and blood pressure check for La Piñata, who, as you will see if you come over to look at this screen, would appear to have passed out. She's in the Country Club Maze right now. And she is, I understand, expected for lunch by a friend on the Beltway starting approximately five minutes ago.' Again, Raul was careful to control his modulation, so as to appear as distant, as unconcerned, as he would for any other customer. 'A bona fide emergency would, of course, require the services of Matron, but I don't like sending her down there unnecessarily. She just doesn't blend into the scenery. Try and get her to send one of her nurses – appropriately dressed, of course, or else she'll faint, too. Remember, the temperature near the tennis courts is over ninety.' Raul looked at his watch. 'And now quickly. Tell me your disasters.'

'Well, first of all, there's this woman who's tracking Sonny . . .'

'Assign her a video tracer,' said Raul. 'Otherwise, let Sonny handle it. He's cool in an emergency. We can trust him.'

'I'm not so sure. I hope you're right. In the meantime, we also have one very freaked-out beau confessor, but when I left the locker room, he seemed to be getting the support he needs to pull himself together. I sure hope so, because the rest of my disasters can all be summarized by the term "booking dilemma". Or, to put it differently, I'm short more than a few good men. Louis I've had to send home. He got badly grazed this morning by an IUD. Eddy is in a panic because I assigned him to a client who turned out to be his ex-girlfriend's mother. If I hadn't been short already, I would have sent him home after that, but with things being as they are, I thought I had to force him to see the day to a close. This has turned out to be a bad move, because he hasn't been able to get it up. This has meant two more disgruntled clients who have further drained my manpower reserves by demanding Retreads.'

'Yes, that sounds worrying. In addition to which, you have the three who had exams or alleged dental appointments. Any chance you might tempt them in for a few hours this morning with promises of overtime?'

'I could try that, yes.'

'Just to be on the safe side, you might also check to find out which of the trainees have had medical clearance. They're not quite tame yet, but they might be just what your disgruntled customers are pining for.'

'Will do,' said Roland, typing out these last instructions.

'But first . . .' Raul's voice cracked.

Roland looked up and nodded — a bit too knowingly, Raul thought. 'Yes, I know,' he said to Raul. 'The damsel in distress.'

Could he tell? Raul wondered. It wasn't exactly worry, it was more . . . professional concern about . . . what she could withstand physically and . . . whether or not he had the right to act on . . . he supposed he could call it . . . privileged information. Had he gone too far? Intruded too much with his personal agenda? These were the thoughts that clouded his smile as he walked into his inner office to greet

Leonie and Sandra, his two off-duty policewomen.

There they were, ogling the new catalogue, so
engrossed, in fact, that – Raul now saw – he could
have spent the entire afternoon in consultation
with his deputy. It was only with the greatest
effort that they were able to tear their eyes away
from it long enough to greet him.

'I hope you don't mind,' he said. 'I've taken
the liberty of ordering up an assortment of salads
and sandwiches which are laid out for us on the
observation deck. But before we proceed – I
take it that you are both planning to stay on
afterwards for a few hours of amusement?'

'Oh, gosh, yes, if there are any beaux free.'

'I'm not sure. Let me just go check.'

Returning to the middle office, Raul informed
his deputy of the new scheduling headache. 'I'm
sorry,' he said. 'But as you know only too well,
this is important.'

'But they're only really interested in each
other. This request for beaux is just a cover.'

'Then arrange the appropriate melodrama, why
don't you? Be creative. If you put your mind to
it, you could even draw upon the acting abilities
of all those beaux you were telling me about
who can't get it up today. Teach them they can

82

pretend about some things, anyway, for God's sake. You'll be doing them a favour.'

'We shall see,' said Roland, suppressing a laugh. 'In the meantime, you might be glad to know we have eight trainees in the clear, and that the damsel in distress is in recovery. Check out monitor number two.'

Feeling his heart begin to pound faster, Raul tried not to move across the room too quickly. There, on the screen, he saw Fiona sitting in front of a mirror in the Roman Baths, while a female attendant brushed her thick, curly hair. She had just had a shower. Her skin was a glowing pink. Her eyes were clear and as distant as ever. For all she gave away, this woman could have spent the morning having a pedicure.

She had recognized nothing ... asked no questions, demanded no explanations ... she was ice ... beyond redemption ... beyond his reach ... no amount of artistry, of manipulation, could break through the hard, smooth surface of her calm ... Why was she here? To prove to herself, to him that she desired nothing ... As his fingers fell to the keyboard, he felt a fireball of hatred roll through him. Running through the instructions for her afternoon entertainment, he saw they were not sufficient for the task at hand. Far too tame! In any event it was a matter of pride – or so he told himself, as he resolved to make a number of changes to her programme that were, even he had to admit it, not quite . . . not a hundred per cent . . . professional.

CHAPTER TWELVE

The Chastity Beltway was a flight of stairs away from the Roman Baths. It consisted of twelve suites, arranged in a semicircle around a marble pool. This pool area was the only part of the Vulcanian labyrinth where women were not allowed to entertain beaux; it was therefore the place where clients who were still breastfeeding received visits from their babies. As Fiona walked in, two of these mothers were entering the pool for a dip with their six month olds. 'After this morning, I'm beginning to wonder about the wisdom of valuing a penis for its length alone,' one mother was saying to the other. 'In the end, I think it's the circumference that makes the experience worthwhile.' 'I don't know,' said the other as she arranged her infant on a float. 'I'm more inclined to

think that the most important factor is musculature.'

Jacqui jumped up from her reclining chair
when she saw Fiona. Shepherding her into her
private suite at the far end of the semicircle, she
said, 'I've ordered lunch to be brought in here,
because the pool is just too noisy.' A young man
with long black curls was already setting out
two glasses of champagne and a bowl of nuts
at the low, round table next to Jacqui's private
jacuzzi. 'I'm going to step in here for another
soak, if you don't mind,' Jacqui said, passing
the manservant as if he weren't even there. She
threw off her robe.

'Oh,' said the manservant. 'Don't do that to
me. I hurt enough already.'

'That's your problem, not mine,' snapped
Jacqui. 'Now quit talking and do your job.'

'But you're just so beautiful!'

'More to the point,' Jacqui countered, 'my
friend and I are hungry. I ordered two Caesar
salads to be brought up at one o'clock and
here it is 1:15 already. Get cracking before I
report you.'

'I'll only go if you promise me you'll reconsid-
er.'

'I'll do nothing of the sort,' said Jacqui. 'You
disgust me.'

Putting his hands on his chest, the manservant said, 'Ouch. That was a body blow.'

'I've warned you for the last time.'

'OK, OK.' He scurried out of the door marked 'Service'.

Jacqui helped herself to a handful of nuts. Nodding in the direction of the service door, she said to Fiona, 'He's pretty cute, isn't he?'

'You think so?' Fiona said dubiously.

'Sure do,' said Jacqui.

'Well, you could have fooled me.'

'I suppose you're referring to the banter. Well, that's nothing. That's just part of the package.'

'And clearly the part of the package you enjoy the most,' said Fiona.

'You bet I do,' said Jacqui. 'I've got to get rid of my hostility somehow. You know what he's done now?' She was referring, of course, to the good-for-nothing married man who had just dropped her. 'He wrote me a letter saying he'd appreciate it if I could arrange not to go to Parents' Evening until the last half hour because he would feel uncomfortable if his wife and I found ourselves in the main room together. And do you know what the real joke is? His wife has been here all morning. She was actually on the rack! I saw her. And so ever since, I've been sitting here obsessing over what I'd

like to do most – go down there and give
her some real punishment and tell her what
her husband's been up to, or bide my time
and tell HIM how SHE whiles away her daytime
hours . . .'

'The wisest course would be to do neither,'
Fiona suggested.

'You would say that, wouldn't you? But the
wisdom of it is another matter. I can't see where
your own famous discretion has got you.'

'If you're referring to the episode I think you're
referring to . . .'

'It was hardly an episode, Fiona. I'm referring
to the Young Apprentice.'

'I'm over him.'

'How can you be sure?'

'Well, how about this? His birthday came
and went without my even remembering. And
that's really something, when you think how
obsessed I was.'

'But don't you feel like there's a gap in your
life?'

'Really, I've been far too weak even to think
about it.'

'Which is exactly why that husband of yours
keeps you weak.'

'I know what you think, Jacqui, but I can't go
along with it. I really was close to dying.'

'You really were made to believe you were close to dying.'

'You don't realize how much that affair ground me down. You keep saying that the attention was doing wonders for me, but that's just because you were hoping it would be my first baby step out of my marriage. Actually, it did terrible damage. It was all take and no give on his part. All he wanted was to be mothered. If I said anything to him that didn't fit the part he had cast for me, he simply didn't hear it.'

'It would have been easier, I suppose, if you hadn't also been having to work with him.'

'I think that from now on, I'll steer clear of attachments and just use this place as and when needed.'

'But where does that leave your soul, dear Fiona?'

Before she could answer, there was a rap on the door. 'Come in,' said Jacqui, reverting to her imperial mode. In walked a new manservant. This one was a striking redhead wearing nothing but shorts and a pair of granny glasses. 'Not you again!' Jacqui complained.

'I just thought I'd try one more time,' said the redhead.

'Well, guess what. You guessed wrong. Clear out of here, you piece of scum.'

'You don't know what this rejection is doing to me,' said the redhead.

'I don't care what it's doing to you.'

After he had left, Fiona asked, 'How many refusals did you buy for today?'

'A baker's dozen.'

'Doesn't it begin to get repetitious after a while?'

'Not for me, it doesn't. Do you know what the best part is? The way they cower when they back out of the room. The fact that they obey me. When I say no in real life, I know I'm stuck either for days of sulking, or at the very best, three quarters of an hour of trying to come up with an acceptable justification . . .'

CHAPTER THIRTEEN

After lunch, Jacqui managed to talk Fiona into going along with her to the Palace of Foreplay. It had looked appealing in the brochure, but the reality was smaller in scale than what Jacqui was expecting. The ferris wheel of bucking broncos was okay – but only just. If they wanted to call it a ferris wheel, they were bound to deflate the libido if all they provided was an apparatus incapable of rising more than thirty feet.

The Hall of Mirrors was another misnomer, because it was not your own reflection you saw in the glass but the reflections of various beaux – all in ridiculous get-ups and all dancing to music that was not, in Jacqui's opinion, quite loud enough to justify their exaggerated movements. She could, if she really stretched her imagination to its outer limits, just see that it might be exciting for some women to reach out for every sixth or seventh mirror to find that – lordy! – it was not a reflection at all this time but a *real male prostitute*! And, no, she didn't have to shut her eyes to make the imaginative leap because she had proof positive in the pair right up ahead of them. These two women took extreme pleasure in goosing the poor bastards whenever they found them. One had a penchant for the armpits, the other for the groin. It was one of those scenarios that made you very, very glad you were not born a man.

The Merry-Go-Vibrator was, she had to admit it, a relaxing, if also a somewhat dizzying, ride. It set her up nicely for the Moonlight on the Bayou. Without having been mechanically relaxed in advance, she doubted that she would have been able to withstand the two minutes of being kissed and fondled in the dark by an unseen boatmate. As it was, she emerged from the ersatz cave feeling titillated and craving more – which is why she decided to risk the Road to Damascus. This, as it turned out, was the one ride of any enduring value. You travelled down a tunnel on a conveyor belt while a host of disembodied hands rippled over your body. Were they real? Or mechanical? It had to be an ingenious combination of the two – but there was a danger in allowing yourself to become too relaxed. Your judgement could follow. Had she been in her right mind, she would have gone straight back to the Beltway after reaching Damascus. Instead, she had let Fiona talk her into going along to the Casino, where she stupidly allowed herself to be strapped on to the roulette wheel, or, to be more precise, trapped inside 19 Red.

To be even more precise, this contraption she now found herself confined to was not a wheel but something closer in shape to the cones you got in airport baggage reclaim halls. The straps – fitted around her torso as well as her wrists and ankles – were too tight, the spinning motion close to nauseating. As for the foam chips – while they did not seem to hurt their targets, they were too large not to provoke a reflex reaction whenever they came hurling in her direction.

The muzzle was no consolation. After Fiona's number (11 Black) came up and she was led off by an unremarkable beau to an adjoining room, Jacqui tried to take her muzzle off so that she could attract the attention of the so-called croupier and get herself off this infernal machine. But the muzzle wouldn't budge.

The enforced prolongation of the ride sent her blood pressure soaring. It seemed to her that she had contrived to get herself trapped in a metaphor for her life. Going around and around in circles, waiting for some asshole to pick her up . . . not only was she a hostage to whim and chance – she was fucking paying for it with her own hard-earned money! She began to growl with genuine fury, and when that didn't work, she focused a silent but seething hatred on the lucky women whose numbers came up instead of hers. It was only gradually that she came to realize that the luckiest woman of them all – the one who was led off to a back room only to be returned to the wheel after a quarter of an hour for a repeat routine within five minutes, only to be released, serviced, restored to the wheel and released again before the half hour . . . was The Wife.

What was she here for? Was the disputed party so different at home that this woman had to come here for her kicks? She longed to ask her.

She decided she would ask her.

Without necessarily revealing her own identity.

But when?

And how?

The solution presented itself when The Wife came out of her third back-room session looking somewhat bow-legged and breathless. This time she headed not for the roulette wheel but for the Hard-On Café, which was located across the corridor. Not long afterwards, Jacqui's number came up. She wrenched her arm out of the grasp of the beau who tried to claim her, yelling, 'You have got to be joking!' and rushed out of the door.

She slowed her pace upon entering the café, then stopped altogether to take in this small, bizarrely furnished temple to the Phallus. There, in the centre, was a gross enlargement of that famous Hittite sculpture of the priapic god. And there, at the bar itself, was a row of smaller priapic figures serving as a soda fountain. The photographs on the walls took the same motif to the edge of obscenity and beyond. But most alarming were the chairs, which had penis-shaped vibrators built into the seats.

Up and down they went, in rhythm to the loud disco music. Only one was occupied. Although she could only see her from the back, she knew this was the woman she was seeking. She took a deep breath and made her way across the room. For the first time since her arrival at the Vulcania, she felt like a huntress. Fuck all those men. They were just excuses. This was her prey for the day.

For a few delicious seconds, Jacqui stood behind her gyrating form. Then, without the slightest premeditation, she reached over to a neighbouring table and picked up the phallic candle. She was about to hit her on the head with it, when suddenly The Wife swung around.

Offering her hand, she said to Jacqui, 'The Other Woman, I presume.'

Jacqui took a step back. She was speechless.

'Sit down,' said The Wife. 'I've been longing to meet you for ages. Let me offer you a drink. There are so many things I've been longing to ask you. And I'm sure the feeling is mutual.'

Fiona, meanwhile, had involved herself in an elaborate game of strip poker – although now that she and her four playmates had lost all their clothes, the operative word had become suck. It had begun with the toes, moved up on the legs to the upper thighs, and had culminated in her lying across the legs of two of the beaux, performing fellatio on one while allowing the other to lick her breast and the two onlookers to masturbate.

It was after she had serviced three out of four that she fell into a short sleep. When she woke up, only the unserviced fourth – the engaging redhead from lunch – remained in the room with her. He asked her if she was in the mood for a wrestle. Why not? she said, shrugging her shoulders. He led her into a trough eighteen inches deep with cubed red and green jelly. They threw each other around in this for five or ten minutes, and then retired to a cleansing jacuzzi, after which her playmate took her out to a platform over the main pool, where he tied them both together with an elaborate bungee rope. For the first few jumps, they skirted the surface of the water. Then, when the penis he had positioned between her legs had grown to its full size, he adjusted the rope so that their next jump plunged them so deep into the water that their feet bounced lightly against the pool floor.

Next came the water slides, after which the redhead suggested a swing on the giant hammock that was suspended from the central dome over the main pool. Here they took turns tying each other up – two soft elastic bands to attach the wrists to one rod, and two to attach the legs to the opposite rod. Being a gentleman (or so she still thought), he let her go first. As she fondled his penis, she was hardly able to control her butterflies, but when she sat down on him, the sensation of fucking in midair made her come almost at once, and when her turn came to be tied up, she came before he even entered her. She was too absorbed in her own pleasure to notice that he had turned her over and was fucking her up the ass. The netting was wide enough for her breasts to poke through the holes. As she looked down into the pool so far below, she was sure that each new thrust would be the one to break the net and send them flying back to earth, but instead of fearing it, she simply wondered if, when they hit the water, the impact would separate them, or if they would hit the pool bottom still joined.

'I have a better idea,' said the redhead as they climbed down the rope ladder into the simulated jungle. 'There's a three-legged orgy going on in one of the private pools. Why don't we join in?' A three-legged orgy, he explained, was an orgy in which a couple tied two legs together and then saw what it could get up to with other couples. 'And sometimes', he said, after they had reached the designated private pool, 'they also join wrists. Or tie their wrists to a pole.' He began to experiment with the cords he had brought with them. Then, apparently for laughs, he tied not just her wrists to a column, but also her legs and her arms and her waist. Standing back, he wrinkled his nose and said, 'I'm not sure about that colour. Let me see what other cords I can find lying around.' Before she knew what was happening, he had left her alone. Five minutes passed. Ten. Fifteen. The lights dimmed. She shouted for help. She heard laughter, first faint and then louder, and faintly menacing. Then the laughter, and the light, faded away altogether.

CHAPTER FOURTEEN

There is nothing like a little darkness.

As she stood there, peering into what looked to be a thick green fog, it came to her that she had wished this on herself. Not today, but years ago, when she was still a student, when she was working at that co-operative, picking watermelons. They had had little to do in the evenings. They had had to rely on their imaginations. Sometimes they had talked about movies they wished they were seeing, or countries they wished they were visiting or half the plot of a book that they took turns bringing to an alternative conclusion. Sometimes it was the meal they would have first when they got back to civilization. That night they had started with visions – not entirely flattering visions – of where they would all be in twenty years' time, and then they had moved on to the most perverse thing they could each imagine enjoying.

There had been nine of them. Three couples who were, like herself, architectural students, and then there was the boy, technically but not yet spiritually a man, whom she had considered her best friend at the time, and with whom she had shared a house for the previous two years. He was a medical student, and his name as Raul. The last member of the party was Raul's ne'er-do-well cousin, Bobby. The night she was remembering was the one she ended up going off with Bobby – this despite the fact that she was engaged to marry someone else. The involvement with Bobby had lasted just long enough to break her engagement. Although she had little goodwill for Bobby, she did at least have him to thank for sparing her from what would have been not just an unhappy marriage, but also a financially constrained one. Unhappily, her involvement with Bobby had also destroyed her friendship with Raul.

During the two years he and Fiona had shared their flat, he, too, had been engaged to 'someone else' – Wilhelmina, a noble and fearless woman who worked with the Indians in Guatemala. Once he had armed himself with the necessary expertise, he, too, planned to join her in the struggle. Until then, he was meeting up with her for brief interludes at his family home in Mexico City whenever their schedules permitted.

Because there was no question ever of his being unfaithful, he was, for the time they lived together, the perfect friend and escort for Fiona. She had confided in him as she confided in no woman – and so he knew that her engagement was more troubled than his, and therefore ought not to have been surprised when she responded to the attentions of his charming and untrustworthy cousin. But he *had* taken offence. On the evening in question, he had stood up at the campfire and denounced her as a whore.

The denunciation was not, strictly speaking, provoked by Bobby, but by the fantasies she had admitted to during the campfire round robin. Apart from Raul, who had refused to participate, saying that fantasies were private matters and that to dwell on them was decadent, the others in the group had come up with scenarios that were far wilder than hers. The ones she had confessed to were recurring dreams, being fucked by a stranger in the dark, only to find out that there were two strangers, lying nude on a hammock while a tennis match went on in the distance, and this – standing tied to a column next to a Roman bath, listening to voices in the distance while the light faded – powerless, wondering what would happen to her, what the men who owned those voices would make her do.

It was this timid little fantasy – devoid of light, sensation, and even men – that had provoked Raul's attack. He had called her a professional victim, had said there was no hope for her if all she could dream of were new, improved chains, had said, as he walked off, that he hoped it actually happened to her one day, so that she found out what it meant to be degraded, so that she found out what an unreconstructed imagination could do to its deserving owner. 'And when that day comes,' he had cried as he backed into the darkness, 'I hope I'm there to watch.'

I hope I'm there to watch. As she recalled these spiteful words, the question mark that had been hanging over her all day turned into a full stop. Just as her dream had come true, so had Raul's. For the first time she struggled against the cords that confined her. They only dug deeper into her flesh. And she asked herself whom she hated more – Raul for devising what she now knew to be his long-awaited revenge – or herself for asking to be caught in his trap, for walking into the control of a stranger's imagination so willingly – to find pleasure not just in surrender, but in paying for it.

What had possessed her? Why had she ever thought this would be gratifying – to hear a rabble approach and, with the returning light, turn into men. To look at the leers on their eight young faces, to hear them laugh as they walked around her, grabbing at her breasts and her cunt, saying to each other, 'And they call this work?' One by one, they rubbed themselves up against her. The eighth boy lingered while the others untied her – because she was still oiled, she slipped out of his grasp and swam into the pool, taking refuge on the island in the middle. 'Go away,' she said. 'I don't want this any more. I've changed my mind.' But this, as far as they were concerned, was simply part of the script. Three of them jumped into the water and headed for her island. While the others cheered, Fiona fended them off, first by kicking them in the face, then in the balls, as they tried to climb up out of the water.

But she could not fend off all three for ever. One boy was finally able to waylay her from behind as she struggled with the other two. The victor pushed her to the ground. When she fought back, his two friends held down her arms for him. She struggled to keep her legs together, but her attacker was too strong for her. His crowd cheered as he worked himself towards climax, and cheered again as he climbed off her. But then there was another boy at the ready, and after him, another. With the fourth, she gave up struggling. She tried to devise some escape for her mind, but for once, she couldn't. She was here, stuck in a fantasy come true. What was happening was sordid, was giving pleasure to everyone in the hall but herself. As the last boys had their way with her, she noticed that quite a few other young men had been watching through a plate-glass window. The lust on their faces puzzled her. What did they see here that she didn't?

The commotion died down after the eighth boy climbed off her. When she sat up, she noticed how sheepish he looked as he swam to the side of the pool to rejoin his friends. In an icy voice, she said, 'So I take it that's all you bright young things can do for me?'

With meek confusion, they nodded, shrugged their shoulders, mumbled yes. 'Well, then,' she said, 'I'll thank you to provide me with a fresh set of pyjamas and a clean, dry towel from those shelves in the far corner.' All eight trotted off to the designated shelves like a troop of scolded puppies. 'Thank you,' said Fiona, as she emerged from the pool. She took the towel from them.

They were so embarrassed that they could

hardly even look at her as she got herself dressed. 'Well,' she said, as she paused at the door, 'a final thanks to the lot of you. You really had me at your mercy for a good fifteen minutes.'

There was a key in the lock on the other side of the door. On an impulse, Fiona gave it two turns and then dropped it into her pocket. 'She's locked them in! That wasn't in the script, was it?' she heard an outraged young male voice cry out. Looking up, she saw her audience from the plate-glass window. 'Well, it is now,' she informed them as she adjusted the thermostat. 'And the play is all the better for it. The best scenes are always improvised.'

The door to the main labyrinth did not have a lock in it, so she did not repeat the performance. And she did not notice that a few of the men from the observation hall had followed her through.

Fiona's mind was elsewhere – and clearer, more directed than it had been for years – when she walked through the door into the manager's inner sanctum.

She found Raul at his desk – and no, it wasn't strange at all that she hadn't recognized him. Then he had had a beard and long hair. Now he was close-cropped and clean-shaven. Then he had had a boyish look. Now he looked haunted.

He was in consultation with a beau – blond,

teary-eyed and muscular – who was dressed, unconvincingly, in a priest's habit. At the sight of Fiona, the fake cleric jumped to his feet and offered her his chair.

'We'll have to continue our talk another time,' Raul told him. 'I'm afraid I have no understudy for you today, so I'm going to have to ask you to stay on in the confessional for the rest of the shift. Do you think you have the stamina?'

'I'll try,' he sobbed.

'Just bear in mind that it's mostly just talk. Certainly the script for Box B does not require that you show your face. As for your views on the role of the whip, I've noted them here and will make sure you are never assigned to Boxes V, W or X.'

Fiona watched Raul's face closely as he spoke to his employee. You would think they were talking about an assembly line in a plant that made running shoes. It was stripped of emotion. And so systematized! She had always thought that she came to this place to indulge in her own secret needs, and that the reason the services the Vulcania offered were so different from your traditional brothel for men was that women were so much more imaginative. But now she wondered if it was because they were so much more pliant, so much more susceptible than men were to the corporate sleaze merchants like this slime of a turncoat of a former friend now facing her.

Who was pretending to be not at all concerned about the upcoming interview. Having said his goodbyes to the reluctant beau confessor, he now turned to Fiona and asked, 'Will you have tea or coffee?' True to character, he did not wait for her answer. Instead he said, 'Actually, it will have to be Constant Comment, just for old times' sake.' He pressed a button on his control panel. The drinks appeared on a sideboard. He had just given out the order to his deputy that he was not to be disturbed, and was lifting his drink to his lips, when she said.

'How do you justify it?'

It seemed to be the question he was expecting. 'I simply remind myself, my dear Fiona, that you were the one who asked for it.'

'I would never have asked for anything at all had I known that I was handing my life over to someone with privileged knowledge – not to mention a grudge.'

'I played fair,' he said, a wave of emotion surging into his voice. 'I told you my name. I gave you ample opportunity to recognize me – even though, to tell you the truth, I was relieved when you didn't. I would have preferred it if you had left today without knowing. After all, this is not the kind of job I was heading for when our ways parted. It's not something I'd like featured in Alumna Records, now, is it?'

'So, what was it, then? What was it that turned you into a monster?'

He didn't answer. He just stared into his cup.

'I suppose you're going to say something clever and self-righteous, like, the proceeds of this place go to support guns for some high-minded liberation army.'

'Actually,' he said, 'this place is owned by a conglomerate. And is headed by a woman. Who keeps as much of the money as she can to herself.'

'Then I suppose what you'll tell me is that at least, having retreated into capitalism, you have chosen the job which illustrates most perfectly how anyone who works within the system is inevitably prostituting himself.'

'I gave up such self-serving subterfuges many, many years ago.'

'Then I suppose you'll give me some sob story about having to support a houseful of pathetic refugees.'

'Not refugees, actually. Just my four young daughters.'

'So,' said Fiona. 'You did end up managing to talk Wilhelmina into having children.'

He bowed his head.

'What does *she* think of your job?'

'She doesn't. She died eighteen months ago.'

'In Guatemala?'

'Yes. It was an ambush.'

'I'm sorry to hear that.'

'It was, in a sense, the way she wanted to go.'

'That sounds quite bitter,' Fiona said.

'She was not a happy woman at the end, I'm afraid. She felt she was surrounded by people of weak character in a situation that tolerated only strength. Her greatest source of disappointment was, as you have guessed already, myself. We were not on speaking terms when it happened. And afterwards, the people running the camp were quick to get rid of me. For a long time I had only been there at her sufferance. After her death, I became a liability. And I didn't want to stay, anyway. I had had enough. But we had never saved any money. Since returning to this country, I've had to scramble to make ends meet. As far as my finances are concerned, this job has been a godsend.'

'So you plan to stay put,' said Fiona.

'I don't see what choice I have.'

'Do your daughters know what their father does for a living?'

'I try to find ways around it. At the moment they're still very young.'

'What will you do when you arrive at a birthday party to find all the mothers in attendance are your clients?'

'Actually,' he said, 'it's happened already.'

'Well, come to think of it, you must enjoy the power of knowing all their secrets. I guess you make a hobby of it, really to get to the core of people, really to know what makes them tick. What a wonderful use of your prodigious brain, Raul. You can certainly be proud of the entertainment you provided me with today. And to remember my secret desires in such detail so many years later! God only knows what you could arrange for me if I had the opportunity to update your data-base! What's it like, Raul? What's it like to know what women like me really want?'

Raul waved his hand as if to fend off a bee. 'It's . . . it's a distraction. Nothing else. I don't care in the end. It's just a game to keep myself from thinking more about . . .'

He looked at her hard and mocking face and lost his composure. He had been intending to say 'my domestic worries', but suddenly the truth flew out, '. . . just a way of thinking less about myself.'

Although he struggled to control it, his breathing became laboured, his cup of Constant Comment began to swim before his eyes. In his confusion, he was not able to protect himself from Fiona's next move.

Reaching out for his hand, she asked, in a softer voice, 'So what happened? What did this to you?'

Involuntary tears spilled down his cheeks.

CHAPTER FIFTEEN

He could have tried to omit at least some of the details and so concealed the truth – not from her so much as from himself. He could have said it was his wife's irreproachable martyrdom that had broken him. He could have said it was her growing and never edited list of grievances against him that had eventually convinced him that he could be no better in his own eyes than he was in hers. He could have told her about the ill-starred affair and the shaming succession of little infidelities. But instead he went straight to the point and explained to her that he had only ever been pretending to be a doctor during his time in Guatemala.

Oh, he knew all he needed to know. That wasn't the problem. He had been brought down by a single mistake he had made at the very end of his time as a houseman. After a hundred hours on duty, he had mistakenly given a patient on the critical list the wrong injection and thereby killed him. He had then compounded his mistake by failing to tell Wilhelmina. He had tried, but the words hadn't come out. They had been at the camp for four years, practising side by side, before someone sent her the tell-tale newspaper clipping.

By then it was too late to tell the truth to the others, or so Wilhelmina decided. And so he had continued to practise medicine under her betrayed gaze. He could easily have remained there after her death, but he couldn't face it. He had lost too many patients – not through incompetence now, but due to understaffing, polluted water and inadequate supplies. There came a point in 'humanitarian' work, he told Fiona, when your well ran dry.

But he did not add what he now saw to be the truth – that he had ruined his life by trying so hard to make it pure. Every mistake he had ever made, he had made because he couldn't accept that the angel and the whore could live inside the same body.

Why hadn't he been able to admit it, when there was still a chance? He had loved Wilhelmina with a love as pure as love can be, but he had adored Fiona, and had ached to touch her in such a way that he knew only now was neither vile nor treacherous. Touch and encircle her the way she was now touching and embracing him. It felt like coming home. It made him feel unspeakably tired, and so, before he knew it, he had fallen asleep.

It wasn't long before Fiona had stretched out alongside him on the *chaise-longue* and fallen asleep, too.

CHAPTER SIXTEEN

And as they slept, Raul's untended garden of desire went disastrously to seed. Roland did his best to cope, but for every crisis he was able to solve, there was another that went out of control. First it was a posse of trainees pounding on Raul's sealed door – in such a panicked and insistent way as to cause alarm amongst the clients at the juice bar. Apparently the Piñata woman had locked eight of their number into one of the private baths. And someone – perhaps this same woman – had turned up the heat, so they were slowly burning up. While he was supervising the handyman with the skeleton keys, the troubled beau confessor burst out of Box B shouting, 'I can't take it any more! I can't take it any more! I can't take it any more!'

Deprived of the inner office, Roland was obliged

to find a way to calm him down in the public space. He found what he hoped would remain a semi-private alcove and tried to show compassion as the beau confessor babbled on about the fantasies he had been forced to listen to during the course of the day. 'I don't know how I am ever going to be able to trust a woman again after this,' he wailed. By now, he had attracted a sympathetic crowd of females who were old enough to be his mothers. 'Not a goat,' they exclaimed. 'Not a donkey twice in one day. And she said she wanted the giraffe to do what?' When the angry confessee abandoned by the fake cleric emerged from Box B and began to make a scene outside the sealed management entrance, these older women convinced Roland that they could give the poor boy the comfort he needed while Roland dealt with this other less interesting disturbance.

There is probably, Roland reflected, no bigger rejection than to have a man you are paying refuse to hear you to the end of your fantasy. So Roland could understand – up to a point – why the abandoned confessee was so enraged. (He was not at all surprised to note that she was Madeline Magenta, the obsessive who had been trailing Sonny.) But he was most worried about her voice carrying, and so it was without giving the matter ample thought that he convinced her to take a two-for-the-price-of-one offer in the showroom of her choice. He pressed two of the trainees into service. As he led them to their assignment, he noticed, with a degree of surprise, that the beau confessor had apparently agreed to be massaged by his six comforters and, even more surprisingly, appeared to be pleased at the attention.

Roland had been intending to stop by again after delivering the disgruntled fantasist and the two trainees to the showroom, but he was once more diverted from his intended course when two women frolicking on separate swings over the main pool collided in mid-air, cracking skulls and falling like dead weights into the water. Fortunately, two of the beaux who were fornicating on the nearby hammocks happened to be certified lifesavers. They both stopped what they were doing and rescued the drowning clients. Unfortunately, the women they left behind pulled the wrong ropes or levers and found themselves dangling awkwardly twenty, twenty-five feet over the surface of the water. It was with a sinking heart that Roland identified them as the off-duty policewomen.

The only thing for it was to call for the crane and suspend a repairman in a seat attached by a chain. He had it all under way in record time – but any feelings of satisfaction he had at his crisis management skills were destroyed when he ventured a look in the direction of the semi-private alcove – where he had left the beau confessor – and discovered that one of his comforters was now performing fellatio. Unprotected fellatio.

He knew he had to get over there before the situation got out of hand, so to speak. But he also had to placate the off-duty policewomen who, though rescued, were still terribly upset. 'Who's on eunuch duty?' he cried out frantically. 'Someone, please, give these women a full English tea on the house.'

By now the in-house emergency squad had arrived to treat the victims of the swing accident, and a different woman was performing fellatio on the beau confessor. But before Roland could get to the scene, he had to deal with a client who wanted to lodge a service complaint. Apparently, all five of the events she had purchased with her 'hard-earned money' had ended in premature ejaculation. Roland was trying to placate her when he happened to glance in the direction of the showrooms to see that the disgruntled fantasist had tied both of her trainees to examination tables and was now about to pretend to castrate them.

Except that it wasn't a pretence. The knife was real. Apologizing to the unhappy customer, he rushed over to the showroom. The door wouldn't give, so he and two bar-beaux had to approach the showroom from the show side and break the glass. He rescued the trainees, whose teeth were chattering, called the guards to detain the fantasist, and called Ingrid on reception to do a police check.

This reminded him of the off-duty police-women. Glancing over his shoulder, he saw that they had no eyes for the English tea now spread before them, as they were kissing each other passionately. Their robes had fallen open to reveal fold upon fold of cherubic flesh. So! he thought. All's well that ends well. Except that his own tragedy of errors was far from over.

For when he got back to the unhappy customer of the five premature ejaculations, he found that she had been joined by two others of her ilk. One had contracted for an hour on the rack. The other had contracted for an hour of discipline. The room numbers had got confused, and now the one who had been needlessly detained on 'those tedious bars' wanted a refund, while the one who had been mercilessly disciplined was threatening to sue.

Raul! Wake up! Roland wanted to say. Instead,

he got back in touch with Ingrid on reception to find out if there was any way of getting into the Inner Sanctum. But she was far more interested in telling him that the police had checked on Madeline Magenta, to discover that she was not the famed journalist at all, but a dangerous sex offender who had been using her name. A police van was now on its way to the Vulcania.

But so was the shop steward of the MPU (Male Prostitutes Union). There were a number of irregularities he wanted to make a formal complaint about. (a) Why were the men in with the sex offender trainees? (b) Why had reception not run a police check on the sex offender before admitting her to the establishment? (c) The emergency cord in the showroom was defective. When was the last time these cords had been routinely checked? Roland's efforts to give the shop steward his answers were hampered by a second complaint – this one from the Chastity Beltway, where someone else wanted her money back. 'I didn't come all this way to watch a bunch of airheads breastfeeding.'

The crowd standing outside the management office was now coming to resemble a vigilante society, so he ought to have been relieved when the woman who had been accidentally whipped put one hand over her mouth and pointed the other in the direction of the Roman Baths, from which a large, middle-aged man in a three-piece suit was now emerging. 'Quick!' she said. 'Hide me! It's my husband!' The shop steward obliged by throwing a towel over her head and leading her into the nearest empty cubicle. It was all very obvious – the only reason the husband didn't see her is that he had also recognized one of the women who was comforting the beau confessor.

By now a number of other women had recognized him, too. 'There's the father of one of my pupils!' 'My next door neighbour!' 'My chiropractor!' These women also dived into the nearest available cubicles. Alas, it soon became apparent from the screams that some of these were occupied.

Trying very hard now to simulate calm, Roland advanced on the angry man. 'I'm afraid I'm going to have to ask you to leave the premises quietly.'

'And if I don't agree . . .?'

'Then I'm afraid I'll have to eject you by force.'

'Force! Hah! What a joke!' he exclaimed, laughing unpleasantly. But then, for once, things went Roland's way. At that same moment, the jealous husband's attention was diverted by the arrival of the two policemen, there to take the sex offender into custody.

Their attention was, in turn, diverted by the spectacle of their two off-duty female colleagues, who were still locked in a desperately amorous embrace over their untouched English tea.

Happily, deliverance appeared in the form of the handyman, who now had the combination for the door to Raul's inner sanctum.

It was so quiet inside that even in his harried state, Roland regretted having to arouse the slumbering pair. But! All dreams must come to an end. Gently, he shook his employer's shoulder.

CHAPTER SEVENTEEN

'What time is it? How long have I been asleep?'
Raul withdrew himself from Fiona's sleeping
embrace to check his watch.

'Not very long, I'm afraid, but long enough for
all hell to break loose.' As Roland ran through
the disasters, Raul returned to his controls and
typed out a few notes to himself. 'Before we go
any further, Roland, I want you to rest assured
that I take full responsibility for all the mishaps
that occurred while I was asleep. You need not
worry about consequences. In fact, I would like
to thank you for your resourcefulness in the face
of spiralling crisis.'

'Thank you, sir.'

'Please. No formalities,' Raul said. 'Now let's
figure out the order in which to deal with things.
I think the sex offender first, don't you?'

'Either her or the husband.'

'Maybe we can find a way of killing two birds with one stone. But first, let's make sure we have given . . .' He looked up at the *chaise-longue* where, a few seconds earlier, he had been asleep in the arms of Fiona.

She was gone . . .

CHAPTER EIGHTEEN

. . . and hurriedly showering in the Roman Baths. Catching sight of the travelling hologram clock, she noted, with some relief, that it wasn't quite as late as she had feared. It was only half past four. She had half an hour to make it to her daughter's school.

She had been hoping to stop off in one of the boutiques upstairs to buy something for a black-tie dinner that was coming up. She had noticed a pair of silk harem trousers that would have been almost but not quite inappropriate, as well as an intriguing asymmetrical hat. A pity she hadn't the time to browse, she thought: a dress purchase would have been a discreet way to hide the expenses of the day. But she discovered, when she got to the check-out desk, that she was to be charged nothing.

'Are you sure there hasn't been a mistake?' she asked.

'It was an explicit command direct from the manager that overwrote your file.'

'I'm not sure if I like that. I don't like to be beholden to people.'

'I could take it up with him now, if you like.'

'No, no, I'm afraid I don't have the time. Which reminds me. I was going to buy something but I think I'm going to have to put it off. Is it possible to visit the boutiques up here without paying a visit downstairs?'

'Of course, Madam. Here's a brochure setting out the full range of our overground services. Most of our shops stay open until ten in the evening, so you may find it more comfortable to do your browsing later, after the rush.'

Certainly the reception rooms were packed at the moment. All the other women with school-age children were also on their way out. There were so many women buying chocolates and flowers for their husbands at the stall near the front that Fiona could hardly make her way through the door.

Outside were the usual scenes one associated with school gates – toddlers refusing to be put into their car seats, slightly older children leaving behind them a trail of cardigans and lunch boxes, a mother and child retracing their steps as they looked for the child's security blanket . . . except that these mothers had a glow to them.

Fiona wondered how they made the transition so quickly.

She herself needed the emptiness of the fifteen-minute drive to her daughter's school. But . . . she could not control her thoughts quite as skilfully as usual. What exactly was she to make of that last episode? The question kept coming at her from unexpected angles. Each time she told herself that there was nothing to make of it at all. It was just part of the schedule of entertainments.

She was glad to see her daughter, instead of numb like she had been for the better part of a year. She was interested for once to hear the details of her day. No one had played with her at lunchtime, Ruth complained. She had, however, received a merit badge for her drawing of a cantilever bridge. Someone had taken her peg off the wall and so she had been sent to the headmistress for untidiness. This wasn't fair because it wasn't her fault.

Ruth's sense of unfairness was further exacerbated when they arrived at Daniel's school and Daniel insisted on his right to the front seat. After hitting each other in their usual way, they asked

Fiona, 'Why are you smiling?' She did not tell them she was smiling because so many of the other women on the same school run had just come from the Vulcania too. That one in the blue Peugeot – Fiona had seen her at the bar, sharing a banana split with a bar-beau. That woman in the new Volvo – she had been in the showroom with the fourposter bed . . .

For once, she was glad, too, to see her house. It didn't seem so tired this evening. The rebelliousness of the colour scheme pleased her. Surveying its impractical layout, she remembered, for the first time in a long time, the joy with which she had deliberately made it so. And that – she told herself – was the point of taking a day off – to cleanse your mind and your body of all its poison so that you could enjoy the life you had made for yourself, instead of succumbing to listlessness and depression . . .

Except . . .

She was halfway through cooking supper – a potato omelette – she had no idea why – the idea had just come to her out of nowhere – when she felt her husband's hand on her shoulder. 'Darling. You're overtaxing yourself. We could have had lamb chops.'

CHAPTER NINETEEN

Back at the Vulcania, Raul had finished the changeover meeting with the night manager and was just taking his last stroll through the subterranean labyrinth. Workmen were hosing down the bar and pool area, while another team was putting a new sheet of plate glass into the damaged showroom. The nets and swings hanging from the central pool dome had been unravelled. The husband had been placated with a voucher for an afternoon at a brother institution. The sex offender had been taken into custody. The accidentally whipped woman, grateful to have been saved from her husband, had withdrawn her complaint. The victim of five premature ejaculations had agreed to a repeat visit, on the house, to be taken up before the end of August. The distraught beau confessor had been granted humanitarian leave on condition that he pay six visits to a counsellor. The policewomen had been too wrapped up in each other even to notice the presence of their colleagues. The other clients had not complained about the noise or the disruption; possibly they thought that the emergency vehicles and personnel were just part of the show.

Upstairs, Veronica was just beginning her first evening acting class. She was lying on a bench on the stage, while one of her (less promising) tutees practised telling her she had beautiful breasts. Raul noticed with some disappointment that there was not a single face in the student audience that was trying to hold back a snigger. He surveyed the bulletin board outside the classroom. It, too, was terminally earnest. 'Make Your Own Certificate X!' exclaimed one poster. Another advertised Karaoke practice, while a third offered brush-up dance lessons for a forthcoming Sixties Night.

The cocktail lounge was full of young men dressed up and powdered to look like sugar daddies, and clients dressed up as B-girls, while in the main hall, the band was practising for the evening strip show. The dancing beaux were already beginning to flit and prance their way through the service entrance. A few had stopped to exchange notes and jokes with the last exhausted-looking stragglers from the day shift. Meanwhile, a steady stream of delivery men carrying crates and champagne and boxes of lobster filed past them.

As Raul let himself out and shut the door behind him, he decided also to put behind him all the events of the day.

Especially the most perplexing one.

These next few hours were the ones he lived for. His four little girls, craning their necks at the front window, awaiting his return ... jumping into his arms shouting, 'Daddy, Daddy,' as he walked through the door ... the housekeeper, finishing her last cup of coffee while she relayed the day's messages, but remaining largely unheard because his girls were all talking to him at the same time ... 'Are you sure you don't want me to stay and help with supper?' asked the housekeeper. 'No,' said Raul. 'The girls and I will manage fine.'

'Get me nine eggs,' he told his eldest, the sombre and delicately pensive Rosa. 'Emmeline, you get out the bowl and after your sister has broken them, you may do the beating. But no arguments, do you hear? Or else I'll change my mind.' Emmeline was a good girl, but she didn't like to take orders, so it was always wiser to start out by setting limits with her, while Teresa, his third, needed to be talked up to – or else she was crushed. The greatest insult was to be taken for her age. So Raul was careful to let her pretend she was in full charge of washing and steaming the new potatoes, while he helped her out invisibly. He gave little Eva the job of finding him a Spanish onion, which he cut and sautéed in olive oil while she went back to search for tomatoes for the salad.

He was making a potato omelette. He knew exactly where the idea had come from – it was the first thing he had ever made for Fiona, that first night so many years ago when she had turned up to talk about sharing his apartment. What he didn't know was why it was so urgent to repeat the meal again tonight – or why, having succumbed to this whim, it was making him so unreasonably cheerful. Chores that usually weighed on him now lifted his heart ... he actually enjoyed the childish bickering over unfair portions and the eruption of bad manners ... even the clean-up seemed quick and effortless. Surveying the immaculate kitchen afterwards, he allowed himself a rare moment of self-congratulation. It had been a difficult year, but he had succeeded in making his family a team. He let bath-time go on for an hour. Then he allowed the girls to talk him into reading them twice as many stories as usual. As they huddled around his rocking chair, he told himself no one else mattered. They were a world unto themselves.

So why, when he had sent them away to put on their pyjamas, did he find himself taking out the phone directory, and looking for her name? Why, having dialled the number, did he just as suddenly hang up? It didn't add up, he told himself as his daughters' laughter filtered in from the bedroom. He needed nothing and nobody. He dialled her number again.

She sounded annoyed when he identified himself.

'If I'm calling at an inopportune time, just pretend I'm a phone bank, selling insurance.'

'I'll do nothing of the sort,' she said. 'What do you want?'

'It's just an idea that came to me. Please do say no if you think it's inappropriate. I just thought, for old times' sake . . . perhaps one day next week, on my day off perhaps, which is Monday . . . we could meet for a coffee.'

There was no answer forthcoming.

'And when I say coffee, I mean coffee and nothing else. I think, now that you know the background, you can appreciate how rare a treat that would be for me, and how sincerely I wish to meet you for a coffee with absolutely no strings attached.'

'I was sure you were going to say ropes,' Fiona said.

Raul could not find it in him to laugh and so remained silent.

'Well . . .' said Fiona after a pause. 'Well, I suppose there wouldn't be any harm in it. I already know the worst of it, don't I? I suppose that's one way to feel safe.'

'Actually,' said Raul without much humour, 'I could say the same about you.'

'If you don't mind my saying so, that's what I meant.'

'Sorry. I'm not too quick on the uptake at this time of day.'

'I can certainly understand why.'

'So. It's agreed for Monday, is it?'

'Monday it is.'

'Ten o'clock at the Phoenicia?'

'Ten o'clock at the Phoenicia.'

Raul put down the phone, went to look out of the window at the hill where he deduced her house was. Then he pulled himself together and settled himself down once more on the rocking chair to read to his daughters. He fell asleep in the middle of singing them a revolutionary ballad. Soon afterwards, he was adrift in his favourite recurring dream, about sitting in a rowing boat in the middle of a lake, with a fishing rod that remained ... for ever ... idle ...

CHAPTER TWENTY

... while a few miles away in the park at the centre of their beautiful city, two couples sat admiring a stately man-made waterfall from opposite shores of the river.

Jacqui and The Wife were perched on a low stone wall. They had run out of stories to tell each other. They had long since established that the man they had been sharing was, to all extents and purposes, two different people. They had also decided that this didn't matter, as both were bastards. In Jacqui's words, the man was the personification of Hobson's Choice.

What they hadn't decided on yet was a fitting punishment, but The Wife was sure they would come up with a good one if they first allowed themselves the luxury of a few double margaritas. 'I know a place that has excellent nachos,' she

said. 'If we go now, we can even hit Happy Hour.'
She put her arm around Jacqui's shoulders as if
to shepherd her. Why, Jacqui wondered, was this
the most titillating thing that had happened to her
all day?

Meanwhile, on the opposite riverbank, Roland
and Sonny contemplated the floodlit waterfall in
silence. What a relief, after a day of amicable
insincerities, just to sit here without trying to
read anyone's mind. What a relief, also, to
know that Sonny was safe, his pursuer behind
bars. How cool Sonny had been about it all.
How rattled Roland was by the intermittent
thoughts about what could have happened if
. . . but it hadn't happened. God's gift to Roland
was still in one big, deliciously muscular piece.
Without stopping to ask for permission in his
ususal self-deprecating manner, Roland reached
out and slipped his hand down the front of
Sonny's shorts.

Now that was what he called muscle tone. And
that was what he called a bone . . .

Fiona, meanwhile, was beginning to regret having
agreed to meet Raul for coffee. Having discovered
Raul's number, she rang to tell him she had
changed her mind, but when a little girl answered
and said he had fallen asleep in his rocking chair,

she changed her mind again. There couldn't be any harm in a coffee, or in meeting under more civilized circumstances, for old times' sake ... he had made it clear that he had even less inclination to discuss what he did for a living than she did to discuss what she had done that day for pleasure.

Why? She hadn't the faintest. All she knew was that it had brought her some peace of mind. She was happy in her body for a change. She needed nothing and nobody. Although today, in addition to feeling purified of toxins she hadn't even known existed, there was underneath it all an inexplicable elation ... a sense of possibilities ... possibilities that were going to open up for her with the seductive inevitability of a blooming flower. Looking around her, she could not blame anyone but herself for this prison she had made for herself. She felt sorry for these people with her, these people whom she had trained to do her thinking for her ... what would her husband do when he discovered this was no longer going to be?

Right now, as they undressed for bed, he seemed intrigued by the spring to her footsteps. 'You're looking especially beautiful tonight, my dear. Whatever you did today, it certainly did you good. Perhaps you should go to that spa more often.'

Once they were in bed, he reached for her. Sometimes, after a day like this, miracles could happen between them. But not today. No, today she had a secret and mysterious hope to cherish. For once, she felt happy, not guilty, to be selfish.

'I'm sorry, darling,' she said to her husband as she turned away. 'I'm afraid I have a splitting headache.'

A NOTE ON THE AUTHOR

Maureen Freely is the author of three novels, *Mother's Helper*, *The Life of the Party* and *The Stork Club*. She lives in Bath.